THE SEEDS OF HAVEN

Jasper Faraday

Table of Contents

Act 1:
The Shadows of Control

Introduction to the Regime

Ethan Hale woke up to the compliance app buzzing on his nightstand. He secretly hated the shrill tone that screamed so loudly in his small, gray-walled apartment. It had recently become the source of his morning irritation. The faint light from the app pulsed in the dim glow of dawn, the bright blue notification demanding his immediate attention. Ethan sighed and reached for it with reluctant weariness. It was the same drill every morning, and the monotony was slowly wearing him down.

Submit your daily loyalty pledge, the screen instructed in bold letters.

Ethan stared at the screen until the words blurred. The pledge was simple enough—a single sentence repeated each morning by every citizen in the Haven community. It should have felt like duty, like purpose. But today, his finger hesitated. The words no longer felt like a mere ritual. They felt like the tolling of his soul.

Still, he couldn't delay. Every citizen submitted their pledge simultaneously, and any delay would raise red flags.

He tapped the button.

"I pledge my loyalty to The Overseers, who safeguard our future," he recited flatly.

The app chirped in acknowledgment, the screen flashed green, and then it fell silent.

Just another pledge on just another day. Another fragment of himself chipped away.

The city of Haven functioned like a well-oiled machine, and Ethan was just another cog. He moved to the window and watched the world stir to life. Everything he saw mirrored the Overseers' cold vision: surveillance drones hovered in the sky like mechanical vultures, red lenses scanning the streets for irregularities. Cameras mounted on every corner swiveled ceaselessly, their glass eyes reflecting the gray monotony of the city.

Ethan returned from the window and freshened up for work. His bathroom matched the lifelessness of his world—dull gray walls, a sad gray tube of toothpaste. His kitchen was filled with sterile, ashen appliances that reminded him of a hospital room. By the time he was ready, he stepped onto the street wearing a plain white shirt, black trousers, and a coat. A faintly blinking compliance badge clung to his lapel.

The badge was both a symbol and a shackle. It tracked his every move and logged every action. He pulled his coat tighter against the chill and merged into the flow of bodies heading toward the Ministry of Order.

The Ministry was a towering structure of steel and glass that seemed to absorb the pale morning light. Its spire reached into the clouds like the embodiment of the Overseers' unyielding presence. Ethan didn't linger. He walked inside, his footsteps muffled by thick carpeting.

His workstation was a narrow desk surrounded by tall screens, each flickering with endless streams of blurred data. His job was to sift through the information—compliance reports, violations, and whispers of dissent—ensuring the machinery of control ran without interruption.

A notification suddenly flashed on his screen:

Compliance Warning: Delayed Submission of Loyalty Pledge.

Ethan's stomach tightened. His brow furrowed as he stared at the flashing message. It was a small warning, but its implications were chilling. The Overseers missed nothing.

He glanced around. No one else seemed to notice. The others were too consumed by their own routines. Still, his heart beat faster. Even a moment of hesitation had been enough to draw their attention.

He dismissed the message and tried to steady his breathing. With trembling fingers, he resumed his work.

But he couldn't stop thinking about the warning. This was the first time he'd been flagged. First time they'd noticed him.

The Overseers weren't people. They were an entity—faceless, omnipresent, and absolute. Every corner of Haven bore their gaze. Every action was analyzed. Every thought felt monitored.

Ethan had grown used to suppressing his doubts, burying them deep beneath layers of compliance. But lately, cracks had begun to show. Today, his hand had hovered over the pledge. Tomorrow, what would it be?

And then, there was his journal.

Hidden beneath the floorboards of his apartment, the journal was a relic from a time when writing was creation—not treason. He'd received it on his sixteenth birthday. Nearly a decade had passed before he dared write in it. Now, its pages were filled with questions and memories Ethan couldn't speak aloud.

His scrawled handwriting filled the margins with thoughts like:

Why do we pledge loyalty to something we never see?

Would we even recognize freedom if we saw it?

The journal was both a refuge and a risk. If discovered, it would mean correction—a word whispered in fear, its consequences unspoken. But for Ethan, writing was rebellion. A way to remember he was still human.

By midday, the sterile silence of the Ministry was broken by the hum of a passing drone. Its red lens scanned the office. When it paused over Ethan's desk, he froze. Then it moved on.

He wasn't the only one who noticed. Faces around him held the same flicker of fear. No one was truly comfortable under the Overseers' gaze.

The rest of the day passed in a blur of data and silence. But Ethan's thoughts kept circling back to the warning. That hesitation. That moment when he'd nearly undone himself.

He walked home under the cold glare of surveillance lamps. The streets were hushed, as if fear had drained the city of its voice. He kept his head down, badge blinking steadily, but couldn't shake the feeling that eyes were on him.

At his apartment, he bolted the door and collapsed into the chair by his window. Reaching beneath the floorboards, he retrieved the journal. The words spilled out like a storm.

Today, I hesitated. It was just for a moment, but they noticed. A warning, small but terrifying. It showed me how little room there is for doubt. And yet, I don't know how much longer I can do this. Every day feels heavier. I'm starting to wonder what would happen if I stopped pretending.

He closed the journal, heart pounding. When had this streak of defiance begun? He wasn't sure. But it was there, growing. He could see himself hesitating again tomorrow. Maybe even on purpose.

He shoved the thoughts aside and hid the journal. Standing by the window, he stared at the Watchtower blinking red in the distance. His fists clenched as a familiar tension settled over him.

For now, he would comply. He would nod, obey, and follow the rules.

But inside, something had awakened. Small. Fragile. But growing.

He shook his head, had dinner, and climbed into bed. Lying in the dark, he let himself imagine—just for a second—what freedom might feel like.

But he couldn't picture it. The idea was too foreign, too distant.

He closed his eyes and drifted into dreamless sleep, dreading the thought of waking up and doing it all over again.

The Price of Disobedience

The next morning began almost identically to the last. The only difference was that Ethan submitted his pledge on time. He didn't want another warning flashing across his screen at work. A second infraction, especially two days in a row, was bound to trigger unwanted attention.

Afterward, he stood by his window, realizing he'd made a habit of watching the city awaken from the safety of his home. The familiar hum of surveillance drones filled the air. Their red lenses swept the streets with mechanical indifference. He had never actually seen one intercept anything, but he imagined their protocols would be swift—and harsh.

Movement near the side of his building drew his attention. It was his neighbor, Lila Simmons, stepping outside with a trash bag in hand. She was quiet, kept to herself, and had always blended into the dull rhythm of their lives. He was about to turn away—until he saw them.

Two Enforcers in black uniforms flanked her. Their expressions were as cold and rigid as the steel batons at their sides. They stopped her, forcing her to drop the trash bag. From his vantage point, Ethan couldn't hear them, but he could see the horror wash over Lila's face.

She glanced toward her building's entrance, and her expression collapsed further. Raising her hands in a pleading gesture, her sorrow was etched deep. But the Enforcers didn't care. One of them pulled out a technological restraint, and they bound her without hesitation.

She was dragged away, begging for mercy.

Ethan pressed his face against the glass, breath caught in his throat. Watching her struggle helplessly, something twisted inside him. The street was full of people—but not one passerby stopped. No one even looked. They just kept walking, like lifeless machines.

Then he saw it.

Above Lila's doorway, the small window meant to display the national flag stood bare. A simple oversight—maybe. But in Haven, such omissions were crimes.

He watched the Enforcers march her to a waiting transport vehicle, their movements robotic and synchronized. Ethan found himself wondering if Enforcers were once citizens—stripped of will, drained of humanity, turned into husks that simply executed orders.

The vehicle door slammed shut with a forceful *thud*, causing him to stumble back slightly.

His fingers gripped the windowsill tightly, heart racing. Lila had been arrested. But why? She was the last person he'd expect to defy the regime. Could she have been a rebel? A dissenter? Or was this simply an example?

Ethan knew the Overseers had perfected the art of making examples out of innocents. Their methods weren't about justice. They were about control.

The image of Lila being dragged away lingered as he made his way to the Ministry of Order. The streets felt quieter than usual. The typical shuffle of citizens had given way to eerie stillness. Perhaps others had seen what he saw—and perhaps it scared them too. Surveillance drones now hovered lower, their red lenses swiveling with sharp vigilance.

He kept his head down, his compliance badge blinking steadily on his chest. Proof of loyalty. Proof of survival.

Inside the Ministry, the too-bright lights and deathly white walls seemed more suffocating than usual. Ethan moved quickly to his desk—his familiar little cage surrounded by towering data screens.

He tried to lose himself in work, but the image of Lila haunted him. He had never witnessed an arrest before. This was only the second time he'd seen Enforcers up close—the first was their inauguration, the second, this.

Midway through the day, his screen blinked with a new alert.

Compliance Warning: Unauthorized Procedural Suggestion.

Ethan froze, fingers hovering over the keyboard. What? He racked his brain. He hadn't done anything out of line.

Wait.

Could it be the minor suggestion he'd made during last week's team meeting? He had casually proposed a small improvement to streamline data reviews. It had seemed harmless—practical, even.

But now it felt like a noose tightening around his neck.

Shortly after the warning appeared, he was summoned to the Compliance Oversight Committee.

The room was as bleak as expected—bare walls, a cold metal table, and a row of screens displaying surveillance feeds. Seated across from him was a small, pasty man: Director Fallon. He looked like someone who hadn't seen sunlight in a decade. Sharp eyes studied Ethan with surgical coldness.

"Mr. Hale," Fallon said, his voice clipped and neutral. "It's come to our attention that you recently proposed a procedural change. Is that correct?"

Ethan swallowed and nodded. "Yes, sir. It was a small suggestion to improve efficiency."

Fallon's lips curved into a smile, but it lacked any trace of warmth. "Efficiency is not your concern. Your concern is compliance. Suggestions like yours indicate a troubling tendency toward..." He paused, then said with exaggerated care, *"independent thinking."*

Ethan's stomach turned. "I didn't mean to overstep," he said quickly. "I was only trying to help."

"Your role is not to help," Fallon said, his tone growing colder. "Your role is to obey."

"But I—"

"This will be your *only* warning," Fallon interrupted, raising a brow. "Further deviations will result in corrective action. Do I make myself clear?"

"Director Fallon—"

"Do I make myself clear?" he repeated, voice sharper.

Ethan swallowed his objections. "Understood, sir."

There was no room to explain, no space to defend yourself. The Overseers were judge, jury, and executioner.

Fallon studied him a moment longer, then exhaled sharply and gestured toward the door. "You may go."

Ethan left slowly, mind spinning. The encounter had been surreal. His footsteps back to his desk felt heavier than usual. Fallon's warning played over and over in his head.

He had always followed the rules. But now, even a harmless comment marked him as a threat.

That evening, Ethan walked home with slumped shoulders. His nerves were raw—fearful, angry, exhausted. Every sound, every flicker from the surveillance drones felt like a warning. He imagined the Overseers watching him, waiting for another mistake.

At home, he bolted the door and sank into the chair by his window. The city glowed with artificial stillness.

He reached beneath the floorboards and retrieved his journal—his one safe place, the only space where his thoughts could breathe. He opened to a blank page and began writing:

Today, I saw Lila arrested. What was her crime? An empty window. Was it intentional? I don't know. Was it just a mistake? Maybe. But it doesn't matter. The Overseers don't need justification. They rule through fear, and we obey because the alternative is unthinkable.

But today, I learned that even obedience isn't safety. I made a harmless suggestion—logical, helpful—and it was treated as a threat. Fallon's words echo in my mind: "Your only role is to obey." Is that all we are? Laboring mules? Silenced minds? Machines in human skin?

I'm tired. I'm so tired. And my breaking point is closer than I want to admit.

He closed the journal and tucked it back beneath the floorboards. Then he stood at the window and stared at the Watchtower, looming red in the distance.

He wondered what it might feel like to resist. What if he had flipped the table during the meeting? What if he had tried to stop the Enforcers from taking Lila?

What would it feel like to truly rebel?

But he shook the thoughts away, forced them back into the corners of his mind. Fantasies wouldn't save him.

One day at a time.

He turned to make dinner, repeating the words like a mantra.

Just one day at a time.

Chapter 3

The Spark of Resistance

The day had begun in its usual dull colors. Haven's sky was an ugly mix of gray clouds, heavy with rain that never seemed to fall. Ethan Hale walked home along the wide, nearly empty streets, his head bent against the cold wind funneling through the towering steel buildings that housed the many ministries of Haven. Overhead, surveillance drones hovered, their soft hum a constant reminder that no movement went unnoticed.

His thoughts were muddled with the monotony of another day at the Ministry of Order. His fingertips still ached from hours of typing, parsing through violations, updating compliance logs, and ensuring that the machinery of obedience remained intact. In moments like these—walking home with only a few others around—he felt most vulnerable. His blinking compliance badge might signal submission, but without the protective anonymity of the morning crowds, it felt like a thin shield. One wrong move, one suspicious glance, and he could be next.

He veered off into a lesser-used alleyway, a shortcut he had relied on many times. The narrow path offered a strange reprieve from the surveillance-covered roads. As he walked, he noticed a man standing beneath a flickering streetlamp. Tall and lean, the man's stillness was eerie. He wore the same gray coat and nondescript trousers as every other citizen, but there was something different in the way he held himself—loose, unbothered, almost at ease.

Ethan slowed as he approached, curious despite himself. There was something unsettling about how calm the man seemed.

"Ethan Hale," the man called out, his voice smooth and clear.

Ethan froze, breath catching. "Who are you?" he asked, voice trembling.

"A friend," the man replied with a slight tilt of his head.

He stepped out from the wall and moved closer. Under the flickering light, Ethan could make out sharp cheekbones, a straight nose, and angular jaws. The man's dark eyes held his gaze calmly.

"Or someone who could be your friend," he added. Then he reached into a satchel slung at his side—something Ethan hadn't noticed before—and pulled out a small, leather-bound book.

"This is for you."

Ethan stared at it as if it were a live explosive. "I can't take that," he hissed, shaking his head. "If they find me with it—"

"They won't," the man interrupted. He stepped closer and gently pressed the book into Ethan's unresisting hands. "Not unless you give them a reason to look. And I don't think you will."

"You don't know me," Ethan said, voice cracking.

The man smiled faintly, his expression softening. "You're right—I don't. But we have more in common than you think. Read the book, Ethan."

Before Ethan could respond, the man turned and disappeared into the shadows.

"Wait!" Ethan called after him, but the man didn't look back.

The book felt heavier than its size. Ethan clutched it to his chest and hurried home, his heart pounding with fear and curiosity.

Once safely inside, he locked the door, drew the blinds, and set the book on the kitchen counter. It was plain, unmarked, its leather cover worn with time. He opened it carefully. A faint scent of aged paper rose from the pages—it had been years since he held a real book.

The title page read: *On Liberty and Tyranny*.

He skimmed the opening lines. The words hit him like a jolt of electricity, each sentence charged with a forbidden energy. The author's voice was powerful and unflinching. Freedom, the book claimed, was an essential, undeniable truth. Tyranny wasn't portrayed as an obvious evil, but as something subtle and creeping—an ever-present force that fed on silence and fear.

With each page, Ethan felt something shift. The words didn't enlighten him so much as unsettle him. They stripped away the numbness he'd built up over the years. The spark of resistance that he'd buried so deeply ignited again, however faintly. But that spark terrified him.

Questioning the Overseers, even in silence, was dangerous. Possessing this book was a death sentence if discovered. He hid it in the same secret compartment where he kept his journal.

But the book weighed on his conscience. Despite the danger, he began carrying it with him—hidden beneath his coat or tucked into the false bottom of his desk drawer. He read it in brief, stolen moments: during lunch, late at night in the dim light of his apartment, or in the quiet corners of the Ministry's vast hallways. When he wasn't reading it, he was thinking about it.

Perhaps it was the book—or maybe it was the mindset it unlocked—but he started noticing more. The way drones hovered too close. The dead stares of his coworkers. The endless, joyless rhythm of the compliance app's demands. It was as though the book had peeled back a layer from his world and exposed the gears turning beneath it.

One evening, as he sat at his table with the book open in front of him, a knock came at the door.

He froze, heart leaping into his throat.

Another knock, louder this time. He stood abruptly, blood roaring in his ears.

He walked to the door and cracked it open, expecting the worst.

It wasn't the Enforcers.

It was the man from the alley.

"You've been reading," he said, peering slightly into the apartment. His tone was calm, not threatening, not friendly either. Just certain.

Ethan stepped back and opened the door wider. The man walked in, scanning the small room with a nod toward the book on the table.

"What do you think?" he asked.

Ethan hesitated. "It's... dangerous."

The man smiled slightly. "Truth always is. But it's also necessary."

"Who are you?" Ethan asked. "Why did you give me this?"

"My name's Marcus," he said with a sigh. "Let's just say I'm part of a group. A fun group, actually. People who see the cracks in the system and want to do something about it."

Ethan tensed. "Like a resistance?"

Marcus inclined his head. "Call it what you like. The point is—we're real. And we're growing."

"You don't know what they do to people like you," Ethan said, voice rising. "They disappear. Their families disappear."

"That's exactly why we fight," Marcus replied, tone firm. "They've taken everything—freedom, choice, even our fear belongs to them. Isn't it time we took something back?"

Ethan looked away, uncertain.

"I'm not asking you to join," Marcus said gently. "Not yet. Just think about it. You've already taken the first step. You've started to question. That's more than most people ever do."

He walked to the door and paused. "When you're ready, I believe we'll meet again."

Then he was gone.

That night, Ethan sat by the window and watched the city drift into uneasy silence. Somewhere out there, the resistance Marcus spoke of was gathering, planning, defying.

He opened the book again and traced the words on the page with his fingertips.

The spark had been lit. And though the road ahead was uncertain, Ethan knew he could no longer ignore it.

Losing Trust in the System

The announcement shook the city the next morning. It rippled through Haven like an aftershock, leaving no room for dissent. It felt like a miniature earthquake, rattling the nerves of every citizen. The Overseers had done many things in their pursuit of "perfect order," but this new decree surpassed them all.

Every citizen was now required to submit to biometric tracking.

The announcement blared from speakers mounted on street corners, and surveillance drones hovered low to amplify the message. Apparently, tracking behavior and speech wasn't enough anymore. The regime now wanted to claim the very essence of life—heartbeat, breath, blood.

Ethan stood at his window, a coffee mug in hand. Through the parted curtains, he watched his neighbors drift through the streets like ghosts. The decree had hit them hard. Their faces were pale, their shoulders hunched, and no one spoke aloud. Even from his apartment, Ethan could feel the tension thick in the air. A collective unease hung over everything.

He turned away from the window and sank into his chair. The book Marcus had given him weeks ago lay open on the table. He had read it cover to cover. Instead of reopening it, he reached for his journal and flipped to a blank page. He pressed his pen to the paper.

They said it was for our safety. They say it's to protect us from threats we cannot see. But the only threat I feel is their gaze, always watching, always waiting. How much more of us will they take? One day, will they take our faces, our movements, our blood, our pulse—our essence? We are not citizens. We are their inventory.

He paused. The pen trembled in his hand.

A faint hum from a passing drone reached his ears. What if they zoomed in? What if they read the words right off the page?

Quickly, he closed the journal and tucked it back beneath the floorboards.

The air in his apartment felt thick, almost suffocating. He longed for freedom—a freedom that lately only visited him in his dreams.

Because of the new biometric registration, work had been suspended for the day. It was a rare reprieve. But that evening, there came a knock at the door.

For a moment, he hoped it was Marcus. It had been a while since they last spoke. But something told him it wasn't.

Ethan's heart beat faster as he moved toward the door. Through the decorative panes, he caught the silhouette of uniformed figures. Enforcers?

He took a deep breath and opened the door.

It wasn't the regime's agents.

It was Caleb.

His brother.

Ethan hadn't seen Caleb in months. Once close, they had drifted apart over the years. Their opposing loyalties had grown into a quiet estrangement.

Caleb looked every inch the model citizen. His posture was straight, almost rigid, and his compliance badge glinted with pride on his chest. He wore his like a badge of honor. Ethan wore his like a brand of shame.

Caleb stepped inside without waiting for an invitation. His eyes—identical to Ethan's—swept the room like they were scanning for rule violations.

"Ethan," he said in a clipped, tense voice. "We need to talk."

Ethan sighed and closed the door. "About what?"

"I'm here to talk about your demeanor," Caleb said, folding his arms. "And your attitude."

"There's nothing wrong with me, Caleb," Ethan replied, voice dull.

"I beg to differ. People have noticed, Ethan. You're not as patriotic as you should be. That kind of behavior is starting to attract attention."

"People?" Ethan asked. "Or you?"

Caleb ignored the question. His voice rose slightly. "This isn't a joke. The new policies are for everyone's safety. Biometric tracking will help identify threats before they happen. Don't you want that? Don't you want to feel safe?"

"Safe from what?" Ethan snapped. "From people like Lila? The woman who forgot to hang a flag and got dragged away for it? Are we really afraid of our neighbors now? Of anyone who dares to think?"

Caleb's face darkened. "Your neighbor broke the law. She wouldn't have been arrested if she had nothing to hide."

"You don't actually believe that," Ethan said softly. "You're not that far gone."

Caleb looked away. For a split second, the rigid mask slipped. Ethan caught something—doubt, maybe. Fear. But it vanished as quickly as it appeared.

"I believe in order," Caleb said, voice steely again. "And so should you. You can't keep living like this, Ethan. People are watching. The Overseers are watching. Keep pushing the limits, and you'll get yourself corrected."

That word. That terrible word. A quiet sentence for a loud punishment.

Ethan looked down, fists clenched at his sides. "Is that why you came? To warn me?"

"I came because you're my brother," Caleb said.

The words should've felt comforting. But they were spoken coldly, like a formality. They barely meant anything anymore.

"I don't want to see you disappear," Caleb added. "But if you keep going down this road..." He let the words trail off, letting the silence fill in the threat.

Ethan turned his back. His voice was calm, but his chest was tight.

"I'm not the one who changed," he said. "You did. You let them take everything from you—your choices, your freedom, your family."

Caleb's face tightened. He stepped toward the door.

"I did what I had to do," he said grimly. "You should think about doing the same."

He opened the door, paused, and looked back one last time.

Then he was gone.

Ethan stood still for a moment, staring at the door before collapsing into the chair. He buried his face in his hands. Caleb's visit had left him shaken. Every time they met, the distance between them widened. It felt irreversible.

He watched from the window as Caleb climbed into his silver car and drove off without a backward glance. Ethan doubted they'd see each other again anytime soon. Maybe the next visit would be through bars—or worse.

He retrieved his journal from beneath the floorboards and opened to a new page.

Caleb came to see me tonight. He spoke of safety, of order, of duty. But all I saw was fear. He's terrified—of losing his place, of losing control, maybe even of losing me. They've taken him. Not his body, not yet. But his will. His free mind. He's part of their machine now, and I don't know if there's anything left of the brother I once knew.

The new policies are just another link in the chain. They call it Biometric Tracking. I call it a leash. They say it's for our safety. But from what? From ourselves? From each other? Or from truths we're not supposed to see?

Ethan closed the journal and returned it to its hiding place.

He leaned his forehead against the cool windowpane and exhaled, fogging up the glass. Below, the streets were dark and quiet. But the regime never slept.

The Overseers had already taken so much. Now, with this new decree, they wanted to reach into the core of what made people human.

And the worst part? He would have to go through the biometric registration the next day. Refusal would mean punishment. Probably correction.

But something in Ethan had begun to shift. The fear was still there—but now, it was joined by something else. A question. A defiance.

What's the difference between living in constant fear and not living at all?

Maybe there isn't one.

Chapter 5

First Acts of Defiance

Haven's cold, biting air hit Ethan's skin as he made his way through the alleyway of the quiet city. He hugged himself tightly to keep the chill from sinking into his bones.

He remembered how, back in childhood, he and Caleb would spend nights like these watching the stars and enjoying the breeze. That memory felt like it belonged to another life. Now, he could barely see the stars through the drone-lit sky, and Caleb's smile felt like a monument to a past long buried.

Tonight, Ethan was out for something dangerous, and the weight of it made him glance over his shoulder repeatedly. He even wore his compliance badge, not to blend in, but because it made him feel like a spy playing a role.

Marcus had left a note—at least, Ethan assumed it was from him. When he got home from work, he found a slip of paper on his table: an address, and a message scribbled beneath it. *You'd want to be there.*

He hadn't overthought it. He didn't dwell on the whys or what-ifs. He simply decided to go.

But now, standing in front of an old, abandoned warehouse, he wished he had.

The distant hum of surveillance drones did little to ease his nerves. The warehouse's metal door was peeling and rusted at the edges, its surface scarred by time. He had no idea how to get in. Maybe there was a secret knock, or a code he hadn't been given.

He hesitated, then raised his hand and knocked three times.

The silence that followed was so absolute it rang in his ears.

Suddenly, a woman appeared. Her sharp eyes scanned him with unnerving intensity, as though she could see every hidden thought. Then, without a word, she stepped aside and let him in.

Inside, the air was thick with the smell of dust and oil. The remnants of heavy machinery littered the space, long since abandoned. A small group of people sat in a loose circle under the dim glow of a single lantern.

"You came," said Marcus, rising to his feet. His voice was low, but welcoming. "I wasn't sure you would."

Ethan nodded, throat tight. "I wasn't sure either."

Marcus gestured for him to join the circle. Ethan sat cross-legged, surrounded by quiet, watching eyes. These people had stepped beyond the line. Just being here was defiance. Yet they didn't look like rebels or criminals. They looked like teachers, workers, parents—ordinary people with extraordinary courage.

He realized, with startling clarity, that he was one of them now.

The meeting began. Voices were soft but confident. They spoke of small victories—disrupted supply lines, a hacked compliance terminal, whispers of resistance spreading in places even the Overseers couldn't see.

But beyond the logistics, there was something deeper—something steady and powerful.

"Why do we fight?" a man asked, his voice rough but calm. "What do we hope to achieve? Freedom? Justice? Or just a chance to breathe without their eyes on us?"

A woman with streaks of gray in her hair answered firmly. "We fight because we must. Because silence is complicity. Even if we don't live to see the world we dream of, we'll plant the seeds for those who will."

Ethan listened, absorbing their words like a sponge. He had expected fury, dramatic speeches, perhaps even shouting. But instead, he found something quieter—stronger. Their resolve didn't burn with rage. It pulsed with clarity, with belief that resistance itself was the point, whether or not it led to victory.

When the meeting ended, Marcus approached him with a paper cup of water.

"What did you think?" he asked.

Ethan accepted the cup and took a long drink. "It's... different than I expected," he said. "More thoughtful."

Marcus smiled faintly. "Rebellion isn't just about tearing things down. It's about building something better. But it starts small."

He paused and fixed Ethan with a quiet, searching gaze. "Now that you're here, what do you want to do?"

Ethan looked around at the others—talking softly in the shadows, laughter tinged with caution. Then he turned to Marcus, eyes steady.

"I want to join the fight."

Marcus folded his arms. "And your first act?"

Ethan hesitated. His hands clenched into fists. "I don't know if I'm ready."

"No one ever is," Marcus said, placing a hand on his shoulder. "But when the moment comes, you'll know."

As he walked Ethan to the door, Marcus handed him a small, black device.

"Keep it on you," he said simply. "Just in case."

The moment came two days later.

Ethan stood in the shadow of a twisted oak tree in Haven's central park. Its bare branches stretched toward the sky like skeletal arms. The park had once been a place of laughter and peace—children running, couples strolling. Now it was little more than a relic, watched and regulated like everything else.

A surveillance camera perched atop a nearby lamppost swiveled slowly, its glass lens glinting in the afternoon light. Ethan imagined the Overseers watching—always watching.

He hated the cameras. Hated how every inch of life was under scrutiny.

And suddenly, he realized—he could do something about it.

His hands trembled as he reached into his coat and felt the cold metal of the device Marcus had given him. A jammer.

He had examined it carefully when he got home. It was crude but effective.

He had dreamed about this moment before. Every vision ended in chaos—drones descending, Enforcers surrounding him, his life labeled and discarded.

But today, he didn't hesitate.

A strange calm settled over him as he stepped toward the lamppost. He moved casually, like anyone else taking a walk, not a man quietly revolting.

He reached the base of the post and looked around. The park was empty. The only sounds were the rustling leaves and the distant murmur of the city.

With a smooth motion, he pulled the jammer from his pocket, pressed the activation switch, and held it to the post.

There was a soft click.

The camera stopped moving. The red light blinked... then died.

For a moment, Ethan stood frozen. Heart pounding. Breath held.

He had done it.

A small act. Insignificant, maybe. The camera would be repaired. The regime would march on. But for Ethan, it was everything.

It was real.

He hurried home, head down, every sense on edge. When he finally reached his apartment, he locked the door and collapsed into his chair.

He read a chapter from *On Liberty and Tyranny*. Then he reached for his journal.

Today, I broke something. Something small. Something they might not even notice. But for a moment, I stabbed them in the eye. And for that moment, I wasn't afraid. That moment was mine.

And that moment *was* his.

He slid the journal back under the floorboards and climbed into bed. The image of the frozen camera played again in his mind.

It was nothing. But it was also the beginning.

And in a world ruled by fear, even the smallest beginning could become something unstoppable.

Act 2:
The Cost of Freedom

Chapter 6

The Regime Tightens Its Grip

The next morning, every screen in Haven lit up at once.

A jolt of fear surged through Ethan as he paused mid-step on his way to work. For one terrifying moment, he thought he'd see his own face. That every corner of Haven would broadcast his image. That he would be named a traitor. A criminal.

But it wasn't his face on the screen.

It was the image of the Overseers—their emblem, a faceless mask against a backdrop of shadowed figures. The broadcast opened with Haven's dreadful anthem, a discordant instrumental that always made Ethan's skin crawl. A burst of static crackled before the familiar breathy voice of a masked figure filled the speakers.

"This is to inform the citizens that dissenters are not merely criminals; they are terrorists. They will be dealt with to the fullest extent of the law. Citizens of Haven, dissent is not an act of courage—it is cowardice. Those who resist the stability we provide seek to dismantle the foundation of our safety. They are not individuals. They are enemies. Terrorists."

That was all.

The anthem played again, and the broadcast ended with the Overseers' emblem filling the screen before fading to black.

Ethan stood frozen for a moment, unsure of what he had just witnessed. The word *terrorist* echoed in his mind. Then, shaking it off, he continued on his way to work.

By the time he arrived, whispers of the announcement were already spreading through the building. At lunch, the topic was still buzzing— an odd thing, considering how rarely anyone voiced opinions in public anymore.

Ethan swirled the bitter synthetic coffee in his mouth, quietly listening to the uneasy murmurs around him. He could hardly believe it. For once, his colleagues—usually silent, robotic—were sharing their thoughts. Their fears.

What's going on in the world? someone muttered.

Back at his workstation, the word still clung to him. *Terrorist.* He'd felt the sting of their accusations before, but this was different. Harsher. He wondered what his coworkers would think if they knew *he* was the one they were warning about.

Later that afternoon, something new arrived—something that caused another ripple through the Ministry.

The Overseers had unveiled a tool. An AI-driven surveillance system designed not to monitor actions, but emotions.

It was called the *Sentience Network.*

Most people, however, simply called it *The Scan.*

Ethan avoided it for days. But avoidance didn't last long. During a mandatory briefing later that week, he finally came face to face with it.

Rows of Enforcers lined the briefing room, standing stone-still along the walls. Their presence left a thick tension in the air. The technician at the front barely registered through Ethan's anxiety as he introduced the system.

The Scan looked unimpressive—sleek and minimal, with a shifting array of lights and soft hums—but its capabilities chilled him to his core.

"The Scan," the technician explained, "uses advanced neural algorithms to detect microexpressions and subtle biometric shifts that suggest subversive intent. It does not replace surveillance. It enhances it. The Scan does not simply observe your actions. It tries to understand your thoughts."

A chill ran down Ethan's spine.

He thought about every flash of frustration he'd felt in the past months. Every flare of anger. Every whispered question. Could *this* thing read those now? Could it parse the doubt behind his eyes? Could it recognize the rebellion stirring inside him?

He glanced around, hoping to catch a flicker of shared fear in someone else's eyes. But the room was a sea of blank expressions.

Except for one.

Mara Lansmith.

She sat beside him, her auburn hair pulled back into a tight bun. Usually quiet, always reserved—just like him. But today, her hands trembled slightly on the keyboard, and her face was pale with tension.

"Mara," Ethan said softly, leaning toward her. "Are you okay?"

Her fingers hovered, trembling above the keys. She turned to him, wide-eyed. There was something behind her gaze—fear, exhaustion, maybe both.

"Do you think they'll really be able to see... everything?" she whispered.

Ethan hesitated. He didn't know her stance. He had to be careful.

"That's what they want us to believe," he replied cautiously.

"What if it's true?" she asked, her voice cracking. "What if they can read what we feel? What if they start—"

She broke off, curling into herself slightly, arms wrapped around her torso.

"Then we'll have to be careful," Ethan said gently, offering her a faint, steady smile. He reached over and brushed his hand lightly against hers. "We'll just have to be more careful than ever."

Mara looked down at their hands. His warmth made her realize how cold her own fingers had become.

"I don't know how much longer I can do this," she whispered. "What choice do we have? They're everywhere. They're everything."

Ethan's touch lingered. He wanted to tell her about the resistance, about Marcus, about the cracks in the system growing every day. He wanted to tell her that just a few months ago, he'd felt exactly the same.

But he couldn't. Not here. The walls had ears. The Scan might already be watching.

"Sometimes," she murmured, eyes distant, "I wonder if it would be easier to stop feeling. To stop caring. Maybe then... maybe then it wouldn't hurt so much."

Her words struck a nerve. He had thought the same once. Considered surrendering to numbness. To just exist. To comply.

But now he understood. To stop caring was to stop being human.

"You can't grow numb, Mara," he said gently. "Caring is the only thing they *can't* take. Don't give that up."

Mara didn't respond. She turned back to her screen, shoulders slumping.

Ethan let go of her hand and watched her breathe slowly, shakily, before she resumed her work.

Her words stayed with him. So did her silence.

That night, as he walked home, he tried to keep his mind blank. There were whispers that drones, too, would soon be equipped with the Scan. No longer just watchers—they would become readers.

And readers of thought were more dangerous than any soldier.

Later, sitting at his kitchen table, the soft glow of the compliance app blinked on his device. Not only did he have to pledge loyalty each morning—now he would have to submit his *mind*.

He thought of the jamming device. Of the camera in the park. Of the word they'd used for him.

Terrorist.

Was it retaliation? Was this their way of reining in the ones who dared to resist?

He grabbed his journal and began to write.

They want us to believe they can see everything. That they can feel everything. But no machine, no algorithm, can truly understand what it means to hope. To fear. To resist. To be human. They can monitor our bodies, our voices—even try to read our thoughts. But they cannot program dreams. And dreams are ours.

He closed the journal and slid it beneath the floorboards. Again.

He didn't know how many times he had done this. It had become a ritual. But this time felt different.

He walked to the window and stared out at the sleeping city.

He imagined a fire—one not of destruction, but of awakening. He saw the citizens rising, bringing down the silver spires, replacing them with color and life and hope.

His reflection glowed faintly against the glass. His eyes were no longer hollow. They burned now, bright with resolve.

He wasn't alone.

Somewhere out there, others were watching too. Others who felt the same. Who would push back, step by step.

The spark within him was no longer flickering.

It was beginning to burn.

Personal Sacrifice

The streets of Haven had grown colder with the changing weather. Ethan wondered when the rain would finally fall—if it did, perhaps it would wash away some of the city's dullness. He moved slowly through the shadows of the road, watching frost gather on the concrete. Maybe snow would come instead.

Even the weather in Haven mirrored its spirit—gray, cold, and lifeless.

The ever-present drones loomed larger now, their lenses bulked with new scanning hardware that made them even more menacing. The coat Ethan wore felt heavier than usual—not just from the cold, but from the slim package tucked in his inner pocket. A parcel from Marcus. A delivery he had to complete.

He hadn't been surprised when Marcus showed up again, calm as ever, handing him the small package and a folded slip of paper with an address. Playing courier wasn't something Ethan had imagined for himself. In another life—before the Overseers—he would have laughed at the idea of smuggling books or data codes like a character in a spy novel.

But now, here he was, walking the same tense path, looking over his shoulder for danger.

What he was doing was madness. He was risking his life and his livelihood. And yet—he had never felt more alive.

The mission was simple: deliver the package to a contact in Haven's western district. The route had been meticulously mapped by Marcus's network of watchers, who would signal when drones passed overhead. Some even created distractions—like walking around without their compliance badge turned on—to buy others time. These were small infractions, but enough to pull the drones' attention. Ethan was amazed by the subtle bravery of it all.

Still, tension pulled at every step he took.

Part of that tension came not from the mission—but from the argument he'd had earlier that day.

Sophia Kingston—his childhood friend from Cares City, Haven's sister city—had visited for a few hours. She worked under the Overseers too, her city a near mirror of his. During their time together, their conversation had turned toward the suffocating weight of the regime. It wasn't long before their opposing views ignited.

"What do you mean a good rebellion would fix things?" she snapped, gripping her cigarette tightly between her fingers.

"Shhh," Ethan hissed, glancing around nervously. They were on the rooftop balcony of his building—Sophie's smoking spot. "I didn't mean it like that. I just think... maybe we can do something. Push back."

She scoffed and took a long drag from her cigarette, then blew the smoke in his direction. "You are fucking unbelievable." Her green eyes rolled as she looked away.

"I just think they're herding us like cattle. And we're not cattle." His voice was tight with frustration. "It makes me furious."

She turned back toward him, eyes sharp. The wind tugged at her curly brown hair, but her gaze was steady. "You're a rebel."

It wasn't a question. It was a truth she had seen in him.

His silence confirmed it.

"You're risking everything," she said, her voice rising. "For what? They always win, Ethan. They *always* win. You've seen it. They crush anyone who resists."

"I know," he said. "But it's not about winning. It's about trying. About showing them they don't own us completely."

Sophia shook her head and turned away. She tossed her still-burning cigarette onto the ground. Ethan moved to catch her eye, but her gaze had gone distant. Her eyes were glassy—he couldn't tell if she was angry or on the verge of tears.

"They've already taken so much," she said, voice barely audible. "Don't let them take you too."

She left him there, stunned and alone.

Her words haunted him even now, as he walked through the abandoned western district of Haven. Sophia had been one of the last connections to the life he'd known before the world changed. That argument would surely be the wedge that drove them further apart.

But what joy was there in friendship when your life no longer belonged to you?

The western district was quieter than the city center—lined with crumbling warehouses and abandoned factories. Windows stared out like hollow eyes. His destination was a rusted storage unit at the edge of the district, marked with a discreet white X.

Ethan approached cautiously and knocked twice.

The door opened immediately. A wiry man with sharp features and an unreadable face stood in the shadows. Ethan handed over the package. They exchanged no words.

Then the man disappeared, and Ethan was left alone with the sound of his own breath.

The return journey was supposed to be uneventful.

But Haven always had a way of reminding you how wrong that assumption could be.

As Ethan crossed a narrow bridge, a sharp whirring sound sliced through the air—the unmistakable pitch of a drone descending.

Panic surged.

He ducked into the shadows beneath the bridge, pressing himself against the damp stone. The drone hovered above, its red light sweeping slowly over the area.

His heart pounded in shallow, stuttering beats. The package was gone, delivered—but in his coat's hidden pocket was still the book. The one Marcus had given him. A single contraband book was all it took to be labeled a dissenter.

Minutes passed like hours as the drone hovered.

Then, finally, it rose into the sky and disappeared.

Ethan's limbs trembled as he stood and forced himself to keep moving.

But the danger wasn't over.

As he turned onto a main street, two Enforcers emerged from an alley. Their black uniforms nearly vanished into the dark. Had he not looked carefully, he would've walked straight into them.

His instincts screamed at him to run.

But he didn't. He knew that would be a death sentence.

He kept walking. Calm. Steady.

"You there," one of the Enforcers barked. "Stop."

He stopped.

The two men approached, eyes scanning him.

"What are you doing out here?" the taller one asked.

"Walking home," Ethan replied as evenly as he could. "I work at the Ministry of Order. I had an off-site assignment."

"Identification," the Enforcer snapped.

Ethan reached for his badge slowly, deliberately. The Enforcer examined it, grunted, and handed it back.

"Move along," he said.

Ethan nodded and walked away, legs stiff, lungs burning. He caught the night bus, blending into the quiet flow of commuters.

It wasn't until he got home that he let himself exhale.

But when he removed his coat, his heart sank.

The false pocket had torn.

The book—gone.

It had likely slipped out somewhere in the city.

Panic clenched at his chest. That book wasn't just paper—it was a symbol. A beginning. A spark. It had pushed open the door to his rebellion. And now, if discovered, it could trace back to Marcus... or worse, to the entire resistance.

He had to tell Marcus. Had to apologize. Had to prepare for whatever came next.

But for now, all he could do was write.

He retrieved his journal. The pen felt heavier tonight, as though weighed down by shame and consequence.

But the words still came.

They told us the city is a machine—that it is forever and eternal. But tonight, for a moment, I slipped through its gears. I lost something important... but I kept something more precious. The will to keep going. They haven't taken that from me. And they never will.

He closed the journal and placed it beneath the floorboards.

Then he lay down in bed, body still trembling from the day's events.

He thought of Marcus. Of the resistance. Of Sophia.

He thought of the cracks in the machine—growing wider, deeper—with each small act.

The future was uncertain. But one thing was clear:

He was just getting started.

Chapter 8

The Power of Fear

The rumors of Lila's release reached Ethan before he saw her.

Lila—his neighbor, the quiet woman who had been arrested months ago for not displaying her fealty flag—was finally back. But when he saw her, she looked like Lila and yet... not like Lila at all.

She had always moved quietly, barely noticed. But now, she looked like a walking ghost. The Overseers had let her go, and Ethan couldn't understand why—they rarely did so without reason. No one left the Overseers' custody unchanged.

He spotted her one afternoon near the derelict market square. Once, she had walked briskly, shoulders back and chin high. Now, she shuffled like a phantom, her steps slow and unsteady. Her frame was hunched, her skin pale and clammy. Her hair, once neatly tied, now hung like a wet mop. Her blue eyes—once filled with quiet life—were empty and cold like ice.

Ethan's instinct was to turn away, to avoid the pain of seeing what had become of her. But something in him resisted. He took a breath and approached her, though his gut twisted with dread.

"Lila," he called softly, offering a hesitant smile. "It's me—Ethan. I live next door. I'm your neighbor."

She turned, slowly, as though the sound of her own name was unfamiliar. For a moment, recognition flickered in her eyes—but it was faint, fleeting. Then it vanished behind a curtain of numbness.

"I... I'm glad you're back," Ethan said, his voice shaking.

She nodded slowly. "Me too," she rasped.

Her voice—once soft and lilting—was now dry and hollow. Ethan hesitated, unsure how to continue. She looked so fragile, so broken.

"Lila..."

"Glory to the Overseers," she said suddenly, with a brittle smile. Then she turned and shuffled away.

Watching her go twisted something inside him. Her image—slumped, silent, stolen—lingered in his mind like a bad dream.

That night, Ethan sat at his kitchen table, haunted by Lila's empty eyes. He reached for his journal, the pen trembling in his hand.

They took her and gave her back—but they didn't return her whole. They stole her fire, her voice, her self. What's left is a warning. This is what happens when you resist. This is what they'll do to Marcus. To me. To anyone who dares to question.

He paused, staring at the ink-streaked page. Guilt twisted in his chest. He thought of the nights he lay awake, aware of her absence, and yet did nothing. He had told himself there was nothing he could do. That her fate was sealed. But now, her shattered return felt like an indictment of his inaction.

I should have done more, he wrote. But what? What could I have done?

He didn't have an answer. He was still running, still hiding. But seeing Lila again didn't weaken his resolve—it strengthened it.

The Overseers responded to the whispers of dissent with escalating violence. Surveillance drones doubled in number, a near-constant presence in the sky. The birds had gone quiet, driven into hiding by the metallic swarm.

The cameras were replaced with sharper lenses, all equipped with the latest Scan technology. The compliance app updated overnight—now demanding not only loyalty pledges but emotional affirmations. Smiles were scanned, tones analyzed, micro-hesitations logged and reviewed.

The rebellion, once bold enough to meet in abandoned warehouses and alleys, now fractured under the scrutiny. Marcus called an emergency meeting in a hidden basement beneath a derelict factory on the outskirts of the city.

Ethan arrived late, nerves raw from a long day of surveillance evasion. The room was dim, the air damp and stale. The group had shrunk—fewer faces, quieter voices.

"We're being hunted," Marcus said, addressing the circle. His voice was grim. "The Overseers know something's happening, even if they haven't found us yet. The new surveillance isn't about monitoring—it's about suffocating. They want us to feel like we can't breathe without them knowing."

A woman scoffed. "So what? Do we stop? Hide? Let them win?"

"We adapt," Marcus said, steady and calm. "We go underground. We spread our message through channels they can't trace. And we survive. Because every day we survive, we weaken their grip."

Ethan listened, his chest tight with both fear and resolve. He thought of Lila's eyes. Of those who vanished. Of Sophia—her fear and her warning. He thought of the journal beneath his floorboards, each word another step closer to treason.

The first step was breaking their old patterns. The resistance dismantled known meeting spots and split into smaller cells. Communications were rerouted through couriers and coded notes.

Ethan's role shifted. His courier missions grew more frequent—and more dangerous. Each delivery felt like threading a needle through a storm. Each time he slipped past a drone or Enforcer patrol, he felt one step closer to the edge.

But it wasn't the drones or the walls or the scans that pressed most heavily on him.

It was the silence.

The silence of Lila. Of Sophia. Of the city. Of neighbors too afraid to whisper. That silence was the Overseers' true weapon—not just their machines, but the fear they had planted in every soul.

One evening, after narrowly avoiding detection, Ethan returned home. He sat in the dark for a long time before reaching for his journal.

Fear is their greatest weapon. Not the drones. Not the cameras. Not even The Scan. It's fear. They've planted it so deeply that most can't even feel it anymore. It's become a second skin. Lila... she's proof of what fear can do. But fear can cut both ways. It can silence us—or it can drive us. Every day I wake up, I choose the latter.

He closed the journal and tucked it back beneath the floorboards.

He wanted to do more—but for now, sleep would have to come.

The next morning, as he stepped outside, he saw Lila taking out the trash. The sight struck him like lightning—a mirror of the day she was taken.

But this time, he didn't hide.

He walked over to her.

"Hi, Lila. Good morning. Can I help you with that?"

He reached out. She paused, then gently handed him the bag.

"Good morning, Ethan," she rasped.

He placed the trash in the bin and turned back to her. She fumbled with the tie of her house robe, eyes curious.

"Have a good day, Lila," he said with a warm smile.

"Ethan..." she called softly.

He turned.

"Thank you," she whispered, a small smile blooming on her lips. It was faint, but real—and it lit up her entire face.

Ethan smiled back and stepped closer. She flinched. He stopped, not wanting to scare her.

"You don't have to thank me," he said gently. "I'm just glad I could help. And I'm so, so sorry you had to go through what you did."

She shook her head and waved him off.

"You don't worry about it," she said. Then she added with a wink, "Besides... I know you're going to do something about it."

She shuffled back inside.

Ethan stood there, stunned—and then he laughed. A genuine, unrestrained chuckle.

He walked to the Ministry that day with a spring in his step. Not even the Enforcers searching him at the gates could wipe the smile from his face.

Because no matter how sharp their scans were or how many drones circled the sky—

They couldn't touch this.

They couldn't touch hope.

Breaking Point

The knock that shook Ethan's door came at dawn.

It was sharp, loud, and insistent—cutting through the stillness of his apartment like a blade. He froze mid-motion as he brushed his teeth, his breath catching. Who would be knocking at this hour? Why now?

Another round of knocks—louder, more aggressive—made him jump.

He rinsed his mouth quickly, wiped down the sink, and hurried to the door. He should've checked first. Should've peeked through the slot. But he didn't. He opened it—and saw two Enforcers standing at his threshold.

They wore pristine black uniforms, their faces as cold and unreadable as the city itself. Between them stood a woman he didn't recognize—sharp cheekbones, pointy chin, a crooked nose. Her dark hair was slicked back into an impossibly tight bun.

She held a small compliance scanner in her hand, its red light blinking ominously.

"Ethan Hale," she said, her tone flat and lifeless. "You are to come with us. Immediately."

Ethan knew better than to argue. Resistance meant violence. Hesitation meant punishment. He nodded wordlessly and stepped out into the hallway. The Enforcers flanked him on both sides and guided him to a waiting transport vehicle.

The ride was silent, but Ethan's mind wasn't. It spun in frantic circles.

Had they found out? Was the resistance compromised? Was it something he did? Something he wrote?

When they arrived, the interrogation building looked like a place where people disappeared. Its walls were lifeless gray, the air still and sterile.

They led him into a stark room with only a table and two chairs beneath a single harsh bulb. They forced him into the chair and bound his wrists with cold metal restraints that dug into his skin.

The woman from earlier entered the room, now carrying a thin folder. She placed it carefully on the table and sat across from him, her eyes fixed on his like she was already dissecting him.

"Ethan Hale," she began in that same mechanical tone. "Do you know why you're here?"

He swallowed. His throat was dry.

"No."

A humorless smile tugged at the corners of her lips. She opened the folder—and there, on top of a stack of neatly printed pages, was his journal.

Ethan's stomach twisted into knots. His eyes flicked from the journal to her face.

"Do you deny it's yours?" she asked, sliding it toward him.

He said nothing. His silence was answer enough.

"We've been observing you for some time," she continued. "Three compliance warnings in a short period. Unusual behavior. Suspicious associations."

She tapped the journal sharply with her palm. "And then we find *this*."

Ethan flinched despite himself.

"These entries," she said, voice lowering, "are treason. These thoughts mark you as a dissenter. A terrorist."

The word hit him like a slap.

His pulse roared in his ears. Cold sweat broke out across his skin. His body trembled—not from the chill of the room, but from fear.

Because this wasn't just a confrontation.

This was judgment.

The journal contained everything. Doubts. Fears. Observations of the Overseers. Veiled mentions of the resistance. A death sentence bound in leather.

"You have a choice," she said after a moment. "Give us names. Tell us who you're working with. Cooperate—and perhaps we can be lenient."

He stared at her, disbelief tightening every muscle in his body.

She wanted him to betray Marcus. The others. Everything he had fought for, everything he had believed in.

He shook his head. "I work at the Ministry of Order," he said quietly. "That's all."

Her expression hardened.

She signaled to the Enforcers.

They unshackled him from the table and dragged him to his feet, escorting him into another room—colder, darker, more terrifying.

And then he saw them.

The tools.

Arranged so neatly it was almost clinical—restraints, electrodes, things with wires and spikes and syringes. Implements of pain. Of punishment.

They strapped him down, made sure he was comfortable.

Then the agony began.

The pain came in waves—sharp, electric, searing. It tore through him like fire. They asked the same questions over and over again, their voices a relentless drone.

Names. Locations. Plans.

Ethan screamed. He writhed. He felt himself slipping in and out of consciousness. But he didn't speak. He didn't give them what they wanted.

Every second felt like an hour. Every hour stretched into eternity.

But through it all, one thought anchored him: *They can take my body. They can take my freedom. But they will not take my will.*

"You can stop this," the woman said suddenly, her voice a smooth whisper by his ear. He hadn't even heard her enter.

"Give us one name. Just one. That's all it takes."

Ethan tried to lift his head, but it felt like stone. His breath came in ragged gasps. He barely got the word out.

"No."

The refusal was soft, nearly silent.

But it carried the weight of every belief he held.

The woman's face darkened. She turned without a word and signaled for the torture to continue.

When it was over, they dragged his broken body into a holding cell and threw him to the cold stone floor.

Every inch of him burned. But he welcomed the pain. It meant he was still alive. Still his own.

He lay there for hours, drifting between exhaustion and consciousness. His mind wandered.

To Marcus. To Sophia. To Lila.

Would they come for her again? Would they arrest Sophia too?

He imagined Sophia crying, furious with him for getting caught. *I told you so*, she would say. *Why didn't you listen?*

And for the first time that day, a cracked smile stretched across his bleeding lips.

They hadn't broken him.

They had tried to strip away his humanity—but they failed. The spark inside him still burned.

When the door finally opened, two Enforcers hauled him to his feet and dumped him outside the facility like trash.

The sunlight stung his eyes, but he held his head high.

His steps were unsteady, but each one was full of purpose.

He was free—for now. But he knew the cost of defiance would come back. The Overseers did not forgive. They remembered.

He made it home.

The apartment was a mess—ransacked and overturned, remnants of the Enforcers' search. But it was still his space. His refuge.

He found the first aid kit and tended to his wounds by the window, wincing as the antiseptic stung his broken skin.

The city stretched before him, a maze of concrete, shadow, and surveillance.

They had his journal now. His words.

But they didn't have *him*.

They could read what he wrote—but they couldn't erase what he believed. They couldn't extinguish the flame.

And they never would.

Bonds of the Resistance

By the time Ethan reached out to Marcus, the man explained that he could no longer stay in his apartment. It wasn't safe anymore.

So they moved Ethan to a safe house.

The safe house was a world apart from Haven's sterile, lifeless streets. Hidden beneath layers of abandoned infrastructure, it felt like a living thing nestled beneath the city's mechanical shell. The air was damp and carried the faint scent of oil and earth—but it was sanctuary.

Here, the drones couldn't reach him. The cameras couldn't see him. And for the first time in a long time, the Overseers' grip felt just a little weaker.

Ethan lay on a narrow cot, his body still aching from the interrogation. Dark bruises bloomed along his ribs like painful purple roses. His wrists were raw where the restraints had bitten into his skin.

But it wasn't just his body that hurt.

The deeper wound was inside—a hollow space carved out by fear, guilt, and uncertainty. What was he supposed to do now? He couldn't go back to the Ministry. He couldn't contact his family or his friends. To the world, he was a terrorist.

And yet, in this sanctuary beneath the city, he waited. He would rest. And when the resistance needed him again, he would answer—no matter the cost.

The door creaked open, and Marcus stepped inside. His silhouette was framed by the dim light of the corridor beyond. He carried a tray with a steaming bowl of soup and a battered book. The spine was cracked from years of handling.

"You look better," Marcus said, setting the tray beside the cot. "Or at least less like someone who's been through hell."

Ethan managed a weak smile and sat up slowly. "I feel halfway back."

Marcus chuckled, placing the book on the table. He pulled up a small stool and sat beside him.

"Halfway's a good place to start," he said. "You've done more than most would."

"It's my honor," Ethan replied with a quiet nod.

Marcus leaned forward, resting his elbows on his knees. "I didn't just come to deliver soup. I came to introduce you to someone. Someone who can help us do more."

Ethan's curiosity broke through his exhaustion. "Who?"

"Dr. Helena Kael," Marcus said. "She used to work for the Overseers. Knows their systems better than anyone alive."

Ethan raised his eyebrows. "She survived *them*?"

"She didn't just survive," Marcus replied. "She escaped. And now she's with us."

After Ethan finished the soup, Marcus handed him the new book—replacing the one he had lost—and helped him to his feet. Together, they walked slowly through the corridors of the safe house until they reached Helena's quarters.

Dr. Helena Kael wasn't what Ethan expected.

Petite, with streaks of silver in her dark hair and piercing golden eyes, she radiated restless energy. Her movements were quick, her gestures abrupt, as though her thoughts moved faster than her body could follow.

She greeted them in a cluttered room filled with monitors, wires, and stacks of handwritten notes. The faint blue glow from the screens bathed her face, giving her an almost ghostly appearance.

Marcus helped Ethan sit down and left without a word.

"You're Ethan Hale," Helena said, skipping any formalities. Her voice was sharp but not unkind. "Marcus told me you're stubborn enough to survive an interrogation and smart enough to be useful."

Ethan nodded cautiously. "He said you worked on their systems. That you know how they think."

Helena smirked. "*Think* is a generous word. Their AI is powerful, sure—but brittle. Built on arrogance and shortcuts. The Overseers trust their tech to do what they can't. That's their weakness."

She gestured for him to follow. Grimacing, Ethan stood and trailed her to a console displaying a web-like network of data nodes.

"This," she said, pointing to the screen, "is the Sentience Network. The core of their surveillance AI. It's vast, interconnected—and terrifyingly efficient."

She tapped a cluster of blinking red nodes.

"But here—this is where their confidence has made them sloppy. Vulnerabilities."

Ethan stared at the map, slowly grasping the scale of what she was showing him. "You're saying we can... break it?"

"Not break," she corrected. "Disrupt. Hit it hard. Flood the system with a virus. Hijack their own channels. Spread our message through their network. Turn their strength into a weakness."

The idea gripped him. That same adrenaline he'd felt when he jammed the park's surveillance camera surged in his veins.

"What are we waiting for?" he said. "Let's do it."

The plan came together over the next few days. It required boldness—and precision.

Helena would guide the operation from the safe house, coordinating small resistance cells spread across the city.

Ethan's role was central. As courier, he would deliver key components to operatives and execute the final upload.

The goal was simple in theory but monumental in scale: upload Helena's virus into the Sentience Network. Overload the system. Hijack the screens of Haven. Broadcast a message of hope.

A message that might wake people up.

Failure meant exposure. Capture. Death.

Even success would paint a permanent target on the resistance.

"Are you ready for this?" Marcus asked the night of the operation.

They stood with the others around a small table, plans spread before them. Everyone's face was grim—determined.

Ethan nodded, his voice steady. "As ready as I'll ever be."

Marcus clapped a hand on his shoulder. "You're not alone. Don't forget that."

The first delivery went smoothly.

Ethan moved through the city like a ghost, ducking drones, weaving between alleyways. The second was riskier—a drone hovered close, forcing him to crouch behind trash bins for several agonizing minutes.

But he pressed on.

The weight of the final device in his coat pocket felt heavier with every step.

At the last drop point, a woman with a scar down her cheek met him in the shadows.

"Good work," she said curtly. "Now get back to the safe house. We'll handle the rest."

Ethan didn't linger. He retraced his route carefully, adrenaline driving him forward. The city lights flickered above him. The air felt charged.

When he stepped into Helena's office, she was already monitoring the network. Her eyes never left the screen.

"It's done," she said.

They waited.

Seconds stretched into minutes. Then—

The screens flickered.

Lines of data distorted.

Then reshaped.

A new symbol appeared.

A bird carrying an olive branch.

The resistance's emblem.

It glowed across every monitor, and—far beyond the safe house—it appeared on the public screens of Haven.

Beneath the symbol, words formed:

Freedom is within you. Do not fear. Do not comply. The Overseers are not invincible.

Ethan felt emotion swell in his chest.

Helena exhaled deeply, her shoulders sagging in relief.

Marcus broke into a smile—a rare, honest grin that transformed his normally stoic face.

"We did it," he whispered.

"They can't ignore this."

Ethan nodded, a grin forming on his bruised face.

For the first time in years, he allowed himself to believe.

The Overseers were not gods.

They could bleed.

The people of Haven had seen a crack in the facade.

They had glimpsed freedom.

The battle wasn't over.

But tonight, they had won.

And for Ethan Hale—

That was enough.

Moral Dilemmas

The aftermath of the resistance attack hovered over Haven like a bruise—deep, dark, and still throbbing beneath the city's polished surface. The air was thick with tension and the hum of ever-present drones. Their searchlights swept across streets still reeling from the chaos that had fractured the illusion of order.

Ethan Hale sat alone in the far corner of the safe house, his fingers trembling as they traced the grain of the scarred wood table. He should have been celebrating. The operation had gone as planned. Helena's virus had spread through the Sentience Network, disrupting the surveillance systems and blasting the resistance's message across the city.

For a moment, Haven had seen a glimpse of something different—something free.

But the cost was far higher than anyone had anticipated.

The Overseers retaliated swiftly, and they retaliated without mercy. Innocent lives were caught in the wave of reprisal. Shops were raided. Families were dragged from their homes. Entire neighborhoods were locked down under the regime's iron grip.

This wasn't what he had imagined. But what had he expected? That a totalitarian regime would simply accept rebellion without bloodshed?

The memory of their terror played in his mind like a broken film reel. He saw a mother clutching her child as enforcers smashed down her door. An elderly man begging for mercy while his home was torn apart.

He closed his eyes.

The images remained.

On the table before him sat a fresh journal—its pages crisp, untouched. Marcus had given it to him after his interrogation, a replacement for the one the enforcers had seized. But Ethan couldn't bring himself to write. Not yet. His thoughts were too tangled in guilt.

Was this worth it?

The question had wormed its way into his mind and refused to leave. It gnawed at the edges of his resolve. *How many more will suffer because of what we've done?*

A soft creak broke through his thoughts. The door to the safe house opened slowly.

He turned, surprised to see Sophia stepping inside.

Her wild, curly brown hair framed her face, catching the low light. She looked different—older, maybe. Tired, but focused. That fire he once saw buried deep inside her now flickered at the surface.

Her green eyes swept across the room until they landed on him, and when they did, a warm, familiar smile lit her face. She walked straight toward him.

He rose quickly, meeting her halfway.

"Sophia," he breathed. "What are you doing here?"

"I came to see you," she said softly, her voice steady but gentle. "There are a lot of things I wanted to say."

Ethan stopped just a few steps from her. "You shouldn't be here," he said carefully. "It's not safe. If you're caught, you'll be branded a terrorist."

"I know," she said, her tone unshaken. "And I understand what that means now."

He blinked, surprised. This wasn't the same Sophia who had shouted at him on the rooftop weeks ago.

"You were right," she added. "We're not cattle. I want to be free."

Ethan winced slightly when she brought up the attack. He had braced himself for her judgment. Her disappointment. But instead, she stepped closer—and her expression softened.

"You gave people hope," she said. "Even if it was just for a moment. You reminded them that the Overseers aren't invincible."

He looked away, guilt rising in his chest. "And at what cost?" he asked quietly. "Do you know how many innocent people are suffering now because of us?"

Sophia ducked her head slightly so she could meet his gaze again. "Do you know how many have been suffering all along, Ethan? Every day, in silence, while we keep our heads down and pretend everything's fine?"

Her words cut through the fog of doubt in his mind.

"I've spent years just trying to survive," she whispered. "But surviving isn't enough anymore. Not when they keep taking and taking until there's nothing left. I'm tired of being afraid."

Her hand found his arm, and her grip was firm, unwavering. "I want to fight. With you."

For a moment, Ethan said nothing. He just looked at her—his oldest friend, his last connection to a simpler past. But she wasn't just a remnant of his old life anymore. She was something new. A partner in this war.

He wrapped his arms around her, his voice a whisper against her ear. "Welcome to the rebellion."

That day, Ethan introduced her to Marcus, Helena, and the others. It felt good to smile again. To watch her move through the safe house, curious and confident, asking questions and taking mental notes. He even made sure her cot was set next to his. Just like old times, but now with a shared purpose.

The next morning, they joined the inner circle in the operations room. The resistance had shrunk—many members forced into hiding after the attack—but those who remained were determined. Their fire hadn't died.

Helena stood before the console, her eyes intense. "The Overseers' retaliation was expected," she said flatly. "If anything, it proves we've rattled them. That's something we can use."

Sophia listened intently, soaking up every word. Ethan felt a surge of pride just watching her.

Marcus laid out the next plan—a coordinated strike to disrupt the Overseers' communication infrastructure. A bold move. A risky one.

Sophia didn't hesitate. She volunteered immediately.

Her resolve sparked something in the room. The morale that had been dragging for days lifted, and for the first time in weeks, there was clarity. Her strength stoked the dying embers of their rebellion.

When the meeting ended, Ethan pulled her aside.

"Are you sure about this?" he asked. "Once you're in... there's no going back."

She looked at him squarely. "I've never been surer of anything in my life."

That night, Ethan finally picked up his pen.

The words came.

Rebellion is never clean. It is never easy. It is a fire that burns bright, but it leaves scars. I see those scars now—in the faces of the innocent, the brave, and the broken.

But I also see the spark that refuses to die. The flicker of hope that no amount of fear can extinguish.

Sophia reminds me of that hope. Her strength, her courage... they light the way forward.

Together, we will face whatever comes.

Together, we will fight.

He closed the journal and tucked it beneath his pillow.

Tomorrow, they would rise again. No matter what retaliation came, the resistance would endure.

And with Sophia by his side, Ethan knew—now more than ever—that they would not face the darkness alone.

Chapter 12

The Attack

The city of Haven seemed to hold its breath as the clock struck midnight. Even the shadows felt alive, stretching and shifting with the movements of those who had chosen to fight for something greater than themselves.

Ethan stood in the center of the resistance's safe house. Around him, the remaining members of the resistance gathered—faces tight with tension, lit by the faint glow of Helena's console. The hum of machines was the only sound.

"This is it," Marcus said, his voice calm but firm as he addressed the group. His gaze moved across the room, lingering on each face as if committing them to memory. "We've worked for months to get here. Helena's virus will take down their surveillance for twenty-four hours. That's twenty-four hours to show Haven that the Overseers can bleed."

Ethan's chest tightened. He glanced at Sophia standing beside him. Her hand brushed his, a simple touch—yet more reassuring than any words.

Helena tapped a series of commands into her console, the screen's glow reflecting in her sharp eyes. "The virus is ready. Once it's deployed, we have to move fast. They'll try to reboot the system, but this—" she pointed to the blinking nodes of the network map, "—will keep them scrambling."

Marcus nodded. "You all know your roles. Stick to the plan, stay sharp, and we'll come out the other side." He paused, his voice softening. "No matter what happens, remember why we're doing this. Freedom isn't given. It's taken. Let's go take it."

The resistance moved like smoke through Haven's narrow alleyways and hidden paths. Ethan's pulse pounded as they approached their first target—a primary surveillance hub disguised within an unmarked building. Helena's virus was already at work, threading through the Sentience Network, disabling cameras, drones, and sensors.

For the first time in years, parts of Haven were blind.

Marcus led the charge. Strong, quiet, unshakable. He was the center of their movement, the thread that held them together. Ethan followed close behind, gripping the small device he was tasked to plant. It would amplify the virus's reach and buy them time.

Inside, Marcus signaled for the team to split. Each member moved to their station. Ethan crouched by a terminal, his fingers steady as he connected the device. Lights blinked in succession.

"We're in," Helena's voice crackled over their comms. "The network's down. Move to the next phase."

Outside, the city was eerily quiet. No drones, no mechanical buzz—just silence.

But the relief was short-lived.

Gunfire shattered the stillness.

"They're faster than we thought," Ethan muttered.

"Move!" Marcus barked, leading them into the shadows of a side alley.

They had expected an hour before retaliation. It had taken mere minutes.

Helena cursed. "They've got a failsafe. I didn't see it."

"How long do we have?" Ethan asked.

"Maybe an hour. If we're lucky."

Marcus gritted his teeth. "Then we hit them harder."

Their next target: a power relay station that controlled much of the city's automated defense systems. Disabling it would stall the Overseers' reinforcements.

As they neared the relay, Ethan spotted a squad of enforcers patrolling the perimeter. Too many. More than they anticipated.

Sophia crouched beside him, scanning the area. "We need a distraction."

"I can loop their patrol feeds for a few minutes," Helena offered, her fingers already dancing across a portable console. "That'll give us a window."

"Do it," Marcus said. "Ethan, Sophia—you're with me."

They slipped past the guards, silent and swift. Ethan's heart pounded in his ears. Sophia worked the explosives while he covered her, every nerve on edge.

"Hurry," he whispered.

"Done," she whispered back.

Marcus set the detonator. "Move."

The explosion was sharp and clean. The station buckled, plunging sections of the city into darkness.

Chaos followed.

As alarms blared, people emerged from their homes—cautious, watchful. The fear that had gripped Haven for so long was shifting, just slightly. They were seeing the cracks.

Marcus exhaled. "We bought them a chance. Now it's up to them."

Helena's voice buzzed through the comms. "System's down. Reboot attempts are failing. We've got hours, not minutes."

Ethan nodded. "Then let's make them count."

But Haven was not done bleeding.

The skirmish came suddenly, a clash of bodies and weapons in a narrow street. Enforcers in black uniforms descended like wolves, their shouts cutting through the noise.

The resistance fought back—desperate but united.

Ethan fired his weapon, the recoil jarring through his shoulder. Every shot was a statement.

Then, an explosion.

It tore through the street like thunder, sending concrete and dust flying. Ethan was thrown back. He coughed, dazed, vision blurry.

And then he saw Marcus—motionless, blood pooling beneath him.

"Marcus!" he cried, staggering to his feet.

Sophia was already there, hands pressed to the wound, her face pale. "He's still breathing!"

Marcus's eyes fluttered. He looked at Ethan and gave the faintest smile. "Don't stop," he whispered. "Promise me."

Ethan gripped his hand. "I promise."

Marcus's fingers went limp. His eyes closed. And the street fell silent.

The survivors returned to the safe house, broken but unbowed.

Helena's face was grim. "The network's still down—for now. But they'll recover. We need to be ready."

Ethan sat in silence. Marcus's final words echoed in his mind. *Don't stop.*

Sophia took his hand. "We'll keep fighting. For Marcus. For everyone."

Ethan looked around at his comrades. Their faces bore exhaustion, grief, and something else—resolve.

The Overseers had taken so much. But they hadn't broken them.

That night, as the city settled into uneasy silence, Ethan picked up his journal and wrote:

Freedom comes at a cost. And tonight, we paid it.

Marcus is gone, but his fight lives on in us. The Overseers think they can crush us with power, but they underestimate the strength of those who have nothing left to lose.

We will not stop.

We will not forget.

And we will not fail.

Seeds of Change

The broadcast room of the safe house was a relic of another time. Its walls were lined with outdated equipment that buzzed faintly—a chorus of forgotten voices waiting to be heard. Dust clung to the crevices of the old console, and the air carried a faint scent of rust. Ethan stood at the center of the room, hand pressed to his chest, feeling the frantic rhythm of his heartbeat. The makeshift console in front of him glowed dimly, wires snaking across the floor like veins carrying the lifeblood of their rebellion.

Helena's voice crackled through his earpiece. "We're live in thirty seconds. Are you ready?"

Ethan swallowed hard. His throat felt dry. "As ready as I'll ever be."

He glanced at Sophia, who stood just behind him. Their eyes met. She gave a slight nod of encouragement.

Turning back to the console, Ethan gripped the table's edge. This was it— their chance to cut through the Overseers' iron grip and speak to the people of Haven without filters, without fear.

The timer on the console hit zero. A faint red light bathed the room.

The broadcast had begun.

Ethan leaned into the microphone. His voice was steady, despite the storm inside him.

"Citizens of Haven," he began, each word sharp, clear, unshaken. "My name is Ethan Hale. For too long, we've lived under the shadow of fear. Our lives have been controlled by those who see us as nothing more than numbers in their system. But we are more than that. We are people. We are voices. And together, we are stronger than they want us to believe."

He paused, inhaled.

"The Overseers have built a machine designed to control and silence us. But cracks are forming. You've seen them. You've felt them. And now is the time to act. Not alone—but together. Unity is their greatest fear. Resistance is their greatest enemy. Let us show them that we are not afraid."

His voice grew stronger. Each word flowed like a river breaking through a dam.

"To the mothers and fathers who fear for their children... to the workers who toil under watchful eyes... to the dreamers who dare to imagine a better future—this is your moment. This is our moment. Rise up. Speak out. Let them see that we will not be silenced."

Emotion swelled in his throat. He faltered briefly, thoughts of Marcus and all they'd lost flickering through his mind. But he steadied himself.

"The Overseers want us to believe that resistance is futile—that change is impossible. But they're wrong. Change begins with us. It begins here. It begins now."

He stepped back, chest heaving. The console beeped, signaling the end of the broadcast.

Helena's voice filled his ear. "It's done. The signal went through."

Ethan exhaled—relief and terror crashing over him. "Did they hear it?"

Sophia stepped forward, resting a hand on his shoulder. "They heard it. I know they did."

The response was immediate.

Across Haven, Ethan's voice spread like wildfire. For the first time, the people heard an unfiltered message—a rallying cry that pierced the veil of the Overseers' propaganda.

In dim apartment blocks, workers paused, their tired hands frozen mid-task as the message played. In the underground tunnels where the forgotten hid from drones, murmurs of hope sparked like embers. In the market squares, where citizens exchanged goods under ever-watchful eyes, the first whispers of rebellion bloomed.

And then came the protests.

Small, at first—clusters of brave souls gathering in alleys, in backstreets. Then, more. In the heart of the city, a crowd began to grow. Hundreds became thousands. Chants echoed, fierce and raw—sounds that hadn't been heard in Haven in years.

The people were waking up.

Ethan watched from the safe house, eyes fixed on the monitors as the scenes unfolded. His heart beat with a fragile mix of hope and dread. The city was rising. Their voices echoed his. But the Overseers would not let this pass unanswered.

Their response was swift. And brutal.

Enforcers stormed the streets, their black armor gleaming under the artificial lights. Tear gas clouded the alleys. Batons slammed against shields. But the crowds didn't disperse. People held their ground. For every protester dragged away, another stepped forward. Fear was unraveling.

Helena turned to Ethan, tension in her eyes. "They'll come for us next. We need to move."

Sophia grabbed her pack. "We knew this would happen. We stick to the plan. We don't let them shut us down."

Ethan clenched his jaw. "They can silence one voice. But they can't silence us all. The people are awake now. And they won't go back to sleep."

As the sirens wailed in the distance, he knew—this was only the beginning.

The Human Spirit

The city of Haven was quiet in a way that felt unnatural—the stillness that follows a storm, heavy and brooding. It was a silence that echoed through the empty streets. Every breath felt as though the air itself carried the weight of what had been lost, and what was still to come.

Ethan sat alone in a small, candlelit corner of the safe house. His mind turned over the events of the past days like stones in a restless hand. He could still hear the distant echoes of gunfire, the panicked shouts, the final words of those who had given their lives to the cause. His fingers absently traced the ridges of the wooden table, grounding himself as memories swirled in his head. The table, worn and splintered from years of use, felt sturdy beneath his touch—a small reminder that something in this world remained unbroken.

Marcus's absence was a heavy and unyielding weight pressing against his chest. It wasn't just the loss of a friend, but the loss of a guiding force who had held them together through the darkest moments. The air felt colder without him, as if the fight had lost some of its fire. The flickering candlelight cast long, wavering shadows on the walls, making it seem as if the ghosts of the fallen lingered still—watching, waiting for what would come next.

Ethan exhaled slowly, his breath a whisper against the stillness. He knew he couldn't linger in grief forever, but in that moment, it felt like the only thing tethering him to reality. He clenched his jaw and willed himself to move forward—to carry the fight for those who no longer could.

Marcus had been their anchor, their North Star in a world twisted by fear and control. Now he was gone, and his sacrifice was a scar that would never fade. Ethan stared at the worn notebook in his hands—Marcus's journal. It had been recovered after the skirmish, its pages filled with scrawled plans, thoughts, and reflections. Flipping through it, Ethan could almost hear Marcus's steady, determined voice guiding them forward, even in death.

"Freedom isn't free," one entry read. *"It comes with a price. And if that price is my life, then so be it. Because the alternative is worse."*

Ethan closed the journal, his hands trembling. He hadn't allowed himself to grieve—not entirely. There was no time for grief in rebellion, not when the fight demanded every ounce of strength they had left. But in the stillness of that moment, he felt its full weight: the loss, the cost, the unyielding resolve it would take to continue. He set the journal down and ran a hand over his tired face.

The fight was bigger than any one of them now. Bigger than Marcus. Bigger than himself.

The resistance was different now—smaller, more fragmented—but somehow, more determined. The protests sparked by Ethan's broadcast had not been extinguished. They had spread. Pockets of defiance lit

Haven like fireflies in the dark. The people were beginning to believe. And that belief was a weapon more powerful than any the Overseers could wield. With each passing day, more citizens whispered words of rebellion. More acts of quiet resistance surfaced. The foundations of control began to tremble.

It was Sophia who broke through Ethan's reverie.

"They're waiting for you," she said gently, stepping into the room.

Ethan nodded and rose to his feet.

In the main hall, more people had gathered than he expected. Recruits—ordinary citizens who had seen enough. Farmers. Laborers. Clerks. Students. None looked like soldiers, but their eyes carried the same fire he'd once seen in Marcus's. They were scared—but ready.

Helena stood at the front, gesturing for Ethan to join her. "This is what Marcus wanted," she said low, so only he could hear. "People fighting for themselves. For each other. You need to show them what's possible."

Ethan stepped forward. His heart pounded like a drum. He wasn't Marcus. He wasn't a leader—not like that. But these people had come to him. Their eyes were heavy with expectation. Their shoulders bore the weight of years of silence. They weren't looking for perfection. They were looking for hope. For someone to remind them that resistance wasn't just desperation—it was necessity.

He swallowed hard and let the moment settle in his chest.

"We do this together," he said, his voice steady. "Not because it's easy. Not because we have a choice. But because if we don't—no one else will."

Training began that night.

Helena's knowledge of tactics and tech, combined with Sophia's sharp instincts, made them a formidable team. Ethan found his place somewhere in between—bridging strategy and spirit, anchoring the resistance in something human.

The safe house became a training ground, a sanctuary for those willing to fight.

"The Overseers rely on control," Helena told the recruits. "Surveillance. Fear. Obedience. They expect us to follow the patterns they've laid out. We weaken their grip when we disrupt those patterns—even in small ways."

A young man—barely twenty—raised his hand. "But... how do we fight them when they have everything? Weapons. Resources. Power?"

Ethan stepped in. "They may have all that. But they don't have this." He gestured to the group. "They don't have people willing to stand together. Marcus used to say revolutions aren't built overnight. They grow in the cracks of oppression. The fact that we're here, asking these questions— that's proof. They're losing their grip."

Someone muttered, "Hope is a dangerous thing."

Ethan met the speaker's gaze. "Yes, it is. And that's why they fear it."

As weeks passed, the recruits hardened—bodies and minds shaped by purpose. They moved unseen. Disrupted communications. Formed small, agile networks. Helena trained them relentlessly, preparing them for the next strike. Sophia led scouting missions. Ethan kept the fire alive in their hearts.

Their victories grew: the drone they downed, the convoy they intercepted, the checkpoint they destroyed. Every success became a symbol—proof that they were no longer scattered. They were a movement.

One night, Ethan stood on the rooftop, the city stretching out before him. The skyline glimmered with cold light, Overseer patrols casting beams across broken concrete. But in the cracks, rebellion bloomed. Lights flickered in patterns. Walls whispered with graffiti. Resistance lived in every corner.

Sophia joined him, arms crossed against the cold. "You're thinking about him, aren't you?"

Ethan nodded. "Every day. Every decision I make, I wonder... is it what Marcus would have done?"

Sophia rested her hand on his shoulder. "He believed in you. We all do. And you're not alone."

He turned to her. "I just don't want to fail them."

"Then don't," she said simply. But her voice carried weight. Her hand tightened around his forearm. "Keep going. Keep fighting. If we stop now, everything—Marcus's sacrifice, our efforts—it'll mean nothing. And I won't let that happen. None of us will."

He turned away, blinking hard, looking out over the city. Haven was broken—but still standing. So were they.

He exhaled, shoulders squaring. "Then we fight. No more hesitation. No more second-guessing. We make every move count."

Sophia smiled faintly. "That's what Marcus would've wanted. That's what we all want."

The first snowfall of the season drifted gently from the sky, soft flakes settling across the rooftops. The cold bit at his skin, but it also soothed. It felt like something new—a cover, a cleansing, a quiet breath between storms.

And for the first time in a long time, Ethan felt something close to hope.

The fight wasn't over.

And as long as the human spirit endured, it never would be.

Chapter 15

The Fall of the Overseers

The sound of the crowds was unlike anything Haven had ever heard. It began as a murmur, a gentle ripple that grew into a roar, echoing off the city's steel and glass. The noise surged like an unstoppable wave, rising and falling as if the city itself had come to life. It was more than sound—it was the pulse of a people who had found their voices after years of silence, an unstoppable force carried on the breath of thousands.

Every footstep added to the rhythm of change, the steady drumbeat of a movement too powerful to suppress. It was a symphony of hope and defiance, a declaration that no regime—no matter how strong—could hold power forever. The energy in the air was electric, charged with the emotions of a population that had long been held captive by fear but now surged forward with the promise of something new. Their voices echoed off every building, shaking loose the last remnants of oppression clinging to the city's walls.

The streets of Haven, once patrolled by enforcers and watched over by cold, unfeeling drones, were now filled with people—faces glowing with joy, determination, and long-denied relief. Parents lifted children onto their shoulders. Friends embraced. Strangers clasped hands in solidarity.

The movement had swelled beyond rebellion. It had become a collective promise—never to be silenced again.

They poured into the streets from every corner of the city. Voices joined in a chorus of resistance. It was no longer just the resistance against oppression—it was the entire city, awakened and unafraid, finally reclaiming what had been taken.

An older woman turned to the young man beside her.

"I never thought I'd see this day," she whispered, awe trembling in her voice. Her hands shook slightly—whether from age or emotion, even she couldn't say. Her eyes scanned the sea of determined faces, the banners waving high, the families standing together without fear. "For years, I watched them take everything from us—bit by bit, like thieves in the night. Our homes. Our voices. Our freedom.

But today... today, we take it back."

The young man nodded, gripping the worn banner in his hands. The fabric was soft from years of careful preservation. He exhaled slowly, releasing years of anger and hope in one breath.

"We've waited long enough. No more hiding. No more fear. We stand together now—and we'll never be silent again."

Nearby, a father lifted his daughter onto his shoulders. She clapped her hands, eyes wide as she took in the scene.

"Papa, what's happening?" she asked.

He smiled, his voice thick with emotion. "We're making history, little one. One day, you'll tell your children about this."

Families walked hand in hand. Old friends embraced. Strangers became siblings in the revolution. Some wept. Others stood still, breathing in freedom like it was a long-forgotten scent. The city pulsed with new life, its heartbeat strong and unyielding. Every step forward was a promise that the darkness would never return.

Ethan Hale stood on the balcony of the safe house, watching humanity surge through the streets. Their chants rose—a song of hope and rebellion that sent shivers down his spine. He turned to Helena, who monitored the movements of remaining Overseer forces from a portable console. Her fingers danced across the screen, tracking the final sparks of resistance from the crumbling regime.

"It's happening," Ethan said, barely above a whisper.

Helena nodded. "The Overseers' forces are spread too thin. They can't contain this. It's only a matter of time now. The Sentience Network is still down. Without it, they're blind."

Sophia appeared beside him, grounding him with her calm.

"We've done everything we can," she said. "Now it's up to the people."

Ethan nodded, but the weight in his chest didn't lift. This moment—this culmination of sacrifice and resistance—felt delicate, as though it could shatter with a single misstep. He thought of Marcus. Of Lila. Of every name etched into memory by loss. Their fight had not been in vain.

The Overseers' power had crumbled not with one blow but through a thousand cracks. A million voices refusing to be silenced. Enforcers had begun to defect. Even regime officials whispered of surrender. The Sentience Network—once their crown jewel—was now their greatest failure, undone by its own arrogance and the persistence of people who refused to give up.

The march to the capital began at dawn.

Ethan walked at the front of a sea of people, their numbers swelling with every street they passed. The first rays of sunlight painted Haven's skyline gold and crimson, shadows stretching behind them like the ghosts of a dark past being left behind.

The city's main boulevard—once lifeless, patrolled by enforcers and haunted by drones—was now a river of hope. They marched with banners stitched from old flags and scraps of cloth, signs bearing the names of the fallen, chants that refused to be ignored.

They marched for their ancestors. For their children. For each other.

When they reached the capital square, silence fell over the crowd. Before them stood the Watchtower, the towering monument to fear and control. Its red lights blinked like the eyes of a dying beast. Once it had cast a long, terrifying shadow. Now it loomed hollow and defeated.

Ethan stepped forward, ascending the stairs as the crowd held its breath. Each step echoed like a drumbeat. At the top, he placed his hands against the heavy doors. The cold metal was scarred and chipped—proof that even the strongest walls could break.

With a deep breath, he pushed.

The doors groaned and gave way, swinging open with a final cry. The sound rang through the square like the last note of a bitter song.

And then—silence broke into thunder.

The roar of the people rolled over him, and Haven changed forever.

As the sun set, Haven came alive with new energy.

Golden light warmed the rooftops. People spilled into the streets, hugging, dancing, crying, laughing. They cleared debris. They painted over the regime's insignias. They lifted their children and kissed the ground. For the first time in years, there was music in the air—real music. And joy.

The resistance, once hidden in shadows, now stood openly among the people. They were no longer warriors but citizens, helping to guide and shape what came next. No one knew exactly how to rebuild, but everyone was ready to try.

Ethan stood on the Watchtower steps, watching the celebration unfold. Sophia joined him, her hand finding his.

"You did it," she said softly, a smile in her voice.

He turned to her.

"No," he replied. "We did. All of us."

They stood together, the weight of the past and the promise of the future wrapped around them like the dusk.

For the first time in years, Ethan allowed himself to believe. Haven would not be a city of fear anymore. It would be a city of hope.

As the stars began to pierce the night sky, Ethan opened Marcus's journal. His fingers brushed the worn pages. He found a blank space and began to write:

Today, the Overseers fell. Not because of one person, but because of many.

Their power was built on fear. We dismantled it with unity.

This is not the end, but the beginning of something new.

Chapter 16

Rebuilding Society

The streets of Haven no longer echoed with the sounds of marching boots or the hum of surveillance drones. Instead, they were filled with the murmur of voices, the scrape of tools against stone, and the laughter of children who had never known freedom until now. The city—scarred, but unbroken—was beginning to breathe again. And at its heart stood Ethan Hale, a man who had never sought power but found himself at the center of transformation.

Ethan stood on the steps of the Watchtower, the same place where he had addressed the city the day the Overseers fell. Now, those steps were dusty and littered with debris—remnants of a toppled regime. But beyond the rubble, the people of Haven were at work. They were rebuilding their homes, clearing the streets, and planting the seeds of a future no longer dictated by fear.

Sophia joined him, sunlight catching in her windswept hair as she handed him a steaming cup of tea.

"You've been standing here for hours," she said gently. "Come inside. There's still work to do."

Ethan nodded, accepting the tea, but lingered a moment longer. He watched the bustling square below. Once broken by the regime, Lila now led a team organizing food distribution, her voice clear and commanding. Helena worked with a group of engineers, their hands smeared with grease as they dismantled the remnants of the Sentience Network. Everywhere Ethan looked, there was growth.

"They're amazing," he murmured.

Sophia smiled. "They're following your example. You gave them hope when they needed it. Now they're showing you what they can do with it."

Inside the Watchtower, the once-imposing chamber had become a hub for collaboration. Charts, maps, and lists of priorities covered the walls. Representatives from every district filled the room, their voices overlapping in debate.

"We need to establish basic services first," said Mara—no longer the shy girl from the Ministry, but a confident leader. "Water, electricity, medical care. Without that, everything else falls apart."

"And what about governance?" asked an older man. "If we don't establish rules soon, someone else will, and we'll be back where we started."

Ethan raised his hand, quieting the room.

"You're both right," he said. "We need to rebuild the city's foundations—but this time, we must also lay the groundwork for something better. A future where no one can hold power like the Overseers did."

He gestured to the charts. "Checks and balances. Accountability. Representation. These aren't just words. They're tools. And we'll use them to build a government that serves the people—not the other way around."

The room murmured with agreement, but Ethan knew the path ahead would not be easy. Rebuilding trust, dismantling corrupt systems, and forging new ones would take time—time they didn't have much of.

The following weeks were a blur of progress and setbacks. Teams worked tirelessly to restore power grids, repair water lines, and establish medical stations. The Watchtower became the city's heart, pulsing with new life. But not everyone embraced the change.

There were pockets of resistance—not from the Overseers, who had fled or vanished—but from those who had benefited under them. Business owners who thrived on corruption. Former enforcers. And those who simply feared an uncertain future.

Ethan faced this head-on during a visit to the southern district. A group of merchants had barricaded a storage facility, hoarding supplies meant for distribution.

"You can't just take what isn't yours!" his brother Caleb shouted as Ethan arrived. "We earned this. We played by their rules!"

"Their rules are gone," Ethan replied calmly. "And so is their corruption. These supplies were stolen from the people—they belong to them now."

Caleb sneered. "You say you don't want power, but here you are, giving orders."

"I'm not giving orders," Ethan said. "I'm asking you to do the right thing. If you won't, the people will take it back themselves."

A long silence followed. Then Caleb stepped aside.

"Fine. Take it. But don't come crying when this whole thing falls apart."

Ethan said nothing. He simply turned to his team and nodded to begin the distribution. He knew his relationship with Caleb would never be the same—and that was a price he was willing to pay.

Incidents like these tested the fragile peace daily. But there were victories, too: a school reopening, a neighborhood organizing its own repairs, a former enforcer stepping up to protect rather than control.

Late one night, as the city settled into quiet, Ethan sat at his desk in the Watchtower, pouring over drafts for a democratic assembly. Sophia entered, setting a plate of food beside him.

"You should eat. And sleep."

"I'll sleep when Haven is stable," Ethan said with a tired smile.

Sophia sat beside him. "You don't have to do this alone."

He met her gaze. "I know. But if I don't keep pushing, who will?"

She reached for his hand. "All of us, Ethan. You said this isn't about one man. Trust them. Let them lead, too."

The next morning, the council reconvened. Ethan stood before them with a decision.

"I can't be the one to lead Haven. It belongs to all of us. Its future should be decided by all of us. I propose we create an elected council—one that represents every district and every voice. A government by the people, for the people."

A murmur of approval rippled through the room.

"And you?" Mara asked. "What will you do?"

Ethan smiled faintly. "I'll help where I'm needed. But Haven doesn't need a ruler. It needs a future."

The applause that followed was not just for Ethan—it was for all of them. For the city they were building together.

In the days that followed, Haven's people laid the foundations for a new future. A city once ruled by fear was now an experiment in democracy. There were no easy answers, only the commitment of those determined never to return to tyranny.

Lila emerged as a true leader. Her sharp mind and fierce determination drove the logistics team—managing food, medical supplies, and even brokering trade with nearby settlements.

"We didn't fight just to survive," she told a crowd during Haven's first public assembly. "We fought to live with dignity. That means making sure no one gets left behind."

Helena, ever the pragmatist, repurposed the Sentience Network. What was once a tool for surveillance became a platform for education and communication.

"The Overseers kept us in the dark," she said. "Our future depends on sharing knowledge—not hiding it."

Sophia, ever compassionate, focused on people. She helped reunite families, organized community gatherings, and worked with children to rebuild the trust that fear had shattered.

"A city isn't just buildings and systems," she said one night, watching children play in the square. "It's people. If we don't heal them, nothing else matters."

Ethan moved among them—not leading, but guiding. A mediator. A listener. A reminder of what the fight had always been about.

Weeks later, the council presented Haven's new charter. Born of collaboration, it ensured transparency, representation, and human rights. Term limits, checks on power, and an independent judiciary were written into its core.

At the charter's unveiling, Lila stood before the crowd and read the preamble:

"We, the people of Haven, declare that our city shall no longer be ruled by fear or oppression. We stand united in our belief that freedom is not a privilege, but a right—and that power must always be held to account. Together, we will build a society that values justice, equity, and the dignity of every individual."

The applause was deafening.

That evening, as the city celebrated, Ethan retreated to a quiet corner of the Watchtower. He opened Marcus's journal and turned to a blank page.

"Haven is rebuilding. Not just its streets—but its spirit. The people have taken the first steps toward something new. It's not perfect, and it won't be easy. But it's theirs. And that's what matters most.

I see Marcus in their determination. Lila in their strength. Helena in their ingenuity. Sophia in their compassion. This city is not just surviving—it is becoming. And I am proud to have played a part in its rebirth."

He closed the journal and gazed out over Haven. The lights of the city sparkled like stars. For the first time in a long time, Ethan allowed himself to believe the future was bright.

Chapter 17

Lessons Learned

The square pulsed with anticipation. Thousands had gathered, filling every corner of Haven's heart. Where the Overseers' banners once loomed, symbols of oppression, now fluttered new emblems of unity and hope. The air buzzed with energy as the city awaited Ethan Hale's voice.

Behind the curtain, Ethan stood still. The past months had been a whirlwind—rebuilding, healing, and striving to shape something better from the ruins. Now, as the city stepped into its new era, it was him they turned to.

Sophia appeared beside him, her calm presence grounding. "They're ready for you," she said, voice soft but sure.

He nodded, inhaling deeply. "Am I?"

A faint smile played on her lips. "You've been ready longer than you know."

With another breath, Ethan stepped onto the stage. The crowd fell silent. Faces—young, old, worn, but hopeful—greeted him. These were the people who had fought, sacrificed, endured. They deserved more than words, but words were what he had.

Gripping the podium, he began.

"Citizens of Haven," his voice rang clear, "Today, we stand not as subjects—but as free people. For years, we lived under the shadow of fear. Our voices were silenced. Our choices stolen. But we rose. We refused to break. And now—here we are."

A wave of applause surged forward, but Ethan lifted his hand, quieting it.

"This victory is not the end. It's the beginning. The Overseers fell not only because of their cruelty, but because they believed their power was untouchable. They thought fear would last forever. They were wrong."

He paused, letting the silence settle.

"But freedom is not a gift. It's not something we win once and keep without effort. It is a responsibility. We must protect it, nurture it, and fight for it—every single day. Complacency is the enemy. Forget the lessons we've learned, and we risk repeating history."

Stillness rippled through the crowd.

"We must build a society that values justice, demands accountability, and listens. This isn't the work of one person. This is the work of all of us. And it never truly ends."

His tone softened, more personal now.

"I've given everything I have to this fight. And now, it's time for me to step back. Haven doesn't need leaders who cling to power. It needs leaders who know when to let go. The future belongs to you. All of you. And I trust you to protect it."

The applause exploded, thunderous and raw. Ethan stepped back from the podium, heart full. He had said what needed to be said. The rest was in their hands.

Lila stepped forward, standing tall.

"Ethan's right. This is our moment to shape. We cannot be passive. Every one of us must take responsibility for the future we're building. The council has been working tirelessly to ensure power stays with the people. We will have fair elections, transparent policies, and a government that answers to you. But that only works if we hold them—and ourselves—accountable."

The crowd murmured in agreement.

Helena joined her.

"Democracy isn't just about voting. It's about staying engaged. We have the tools to ensure no one ever wields unchecked power again. The Sentience Network is being repurposed—not to control, but to give every citizen a voice. No one will be silenced."

Sophia stepped forward.

"And we must care for one another. Change isn't only about systems and laws—it's about people. Rebuilding trust, healing wounds, and ensuring no one is left behind. This city belongs to all of us. And we will rise together."

Cheers rose again—hopeful, defiant, alive.

Ethan watched the crowd not as a leader, but as one of them. Not as subjects waiting for orders, but as free people ready to take charge of their future.

As the sun dipped low, the square lingered with life—conversations, plans, laughter. For the first time in years, Haven pulsed with joy.

Ethan slipped from the stage into the crowd, listening. He heard conviction in their voices, saw hope in their eyes.

Sophia found him and linked her arm through his.

"You did it," she said.

He shook his head gently. "No. They did."

She smiled. "Then let's see what they do next."

Ethan looked up. Stars blinked into the twilight. The future was uncertain, the road ahead long. But tonight, for the first time in a long time, he allowed himself to believe.

Hope had taken root in Haven—and if nurtured, it would never die.

Later that night, Ethan sat on the Watchtower steps—his favorite place to watch the city. The streets echoed with laughter and music. Fires glowed in the square, warming the faces of children dancing, of workers resting, of families rediscovering joy.

Sophia joined him, silent, a cup of tea in each hand. She passed him one, wordlessly.

"You're leaving, aren't you?" she asked, sadness in her voice, though not surprise.

He nodded slowly. "Yes. Haven doesn't need me anymore. They have Lila, Helena... so many others. They'll be just fine."

Sophia tilted her head, studying him. "And you? What will *you* do?"

He hesitated. Not for lack of answers—but too many. His life had been forged by war, by purpose born of resistance. Without that fight... who was he?

"I don't know," he admitted. "For so long, all I knew was the struggle. But now... I think I want to live. To find peace. To understand what freedom really means."

She reached for his hand, her touch steady.

"You've earned that. But you'll be missed."

He turned toward her, eyes soft. "I'll miss you too. More than you know."

At dawn, Ethan stood in the Watchtower's quiet quarters, packing a small bag. He owned little—just clothes, a knife, a battered map. On top, he laid Marcus's journal before pulling the strap shut.

He paused, taking in the room. Scars of war still marked the walls—bullet holes, scorch marks. But on the windowsill, a plant Sophia had placed had begun to bloom. Even here, life had found a way.

With the bag slung over his shoulder, he stepped into the still-sleeping city. The streets once guarded by Overseers were peaceful, reclaimed by the people.

He passed a toppled statue, a burned checkpoint, slogans half-faded on cracked walls. The past remained—but it no longer ruled.

At the northern gate, he stopped. The horizon stretched wide, infinite.

Ethan pulled out Marcus's journal and flipped through its worn pages—notes from the resistance, names of the fallen, sketches of rebellion. Then, he found a blank page.

And he wrote:

The fight is over, but the work continues. Haven is free, but freedom is fragile. I leave this city in the hands of its people, trusting they will protect it, nurture it, and carry it forward. As for me, I carry the lessons I've learned, the memories of those we lost, and the hope of what lies ahead. This is not an ending. It is a beginning.

He tucked the journal away.

A voice behind him made him turn.

"You're really going, then?"

Lila stood nearby, arms crossed, her gaze softened by understanding. She was no longer the girl in the dark apartment. She was a leader now. And she would be a good one.

Ethan nodded. "Yeah. It's time."

She stepped closer, extending her hand.

"Thank you. For everything."

He grasped her hand firmly. "It was never just me. It was all of us."

She smiled—and for once, the smile was light, unburdened.

"Be safe out there."

"You too."

Epilogue: The Eternal Flame

The sun rose over the hills surrounding Haven, its golden light spilling across the city like molten fire. The market square bustled with voices and laughter, the air rich with the scent of fresh bread and the earthy aroma of potted plants adorning every corner. Children darted between stalls, their joyous shouts weaving a melody into the morning air. This was a city reborn—a place where hope had not only survived but flourished.

Perched on a hill at the city's edge, Ethan watched as dawn touched the streets below. He sat beneath a mighty oak, its branches swaying gently in the breeze, whispering ancient tales through rustling leaves. A weathered leather journal rested in his lap—a living record of years marked by struggle, ambition, and the indomitable resilience of the human spirit. This moment was his. A time to sift through memories and add the final words to a story that no longer belonged to him alone.

He opened the journal and ran his fingers across the smudged ink of familiar pages. Then he began to write:

It has been five years since Haven reclaimed its freedom. Five years since the people of this city stood together and said, 'No more.' Today, as I look out over the streets that once bore the weight of oppression, I see more than a rebuilt city. I see a renewed spirit. Haven is alive. It breathes. It dreams. It grows.

He paused, watching a group of children playing in the field below. They chased each other with wild abandon, their laughter carried on the wind. He smiled, and returned to the page.

The children of Haven will never know the world we endured. They will grow up in freedom, their paths unmarked by the shadows that once haunted these streets. But they will know our stories. They will learn of sacrifice, courage, and hope. And in those stories, they will find the strength to protect what we've built.

Since leaving the Watchtower, Ethan had found solace in the quiet edges of the city. The oak tree had become his sanctuary—a place of reflection without the weight of leadership. He lived in a small cottage beyond the main roads, where life slowed to the gentle rhythm of nature. He tended a garden. His hands, rough from soil, no longer gripped weapons. And in that simplicity, he had found peace.

Still, the city's heartbeat remained a part of him. Visitors came often—bringing news, seeking guidance. Lila, now a respected council leader, came frequently. Her voice, steady and strong, guided Haven through the challenges of self-governance. The fire that had driven her during the resistance still burned, tempered now by wisdom and resolve.

Helena, ever brilliant, had turned her mind to education. She built schools where children learned not only science and math, but the history of their city and the values it stood for. She repurposed the remnants of the Sentience Network—not for control, but for connection. Technology served the people now. And in every classroom, she taught that knowledge must never again be wielded as a weapon.

Sophia visited the most. She never stayed long, but each time brought warmth and familiarity—a reminder of the bonds forged in rebellion. She spoke of the council's triumphs and missteps, of a city growing into its freedom. More than once, she'd asked Ethan to return. But he always declined, knowing Haven no longer needed him. It had found its own strength.

One evening, as the sun bled into the horizon, Sophia sat beside him under the oak tree. The sky flamed with shades of orange and crimson, reflecting in her green eyes.

"Do you ever regret stepping away?" she asked gently.

Ethan shook his head. "No. My time as a leader ended the moment Haven no longer needed someone to fight for it. Now, it needs people to build it—and nurture it. You, Lila, Helena—you're doing that. And doing it well."

Sophia studied him quietly before nodding. "You're at peace with it."

He exhaled slowly, letting the evening breeze carry away the last of his doubt. "I am. For the first time in a long time, I am."

They sat in silence, watching city lights flicker on, one by one. Once a dream—now a reality. A city free, no longer chained by fear.

As the stars emerged, Ethan turned to his journal and wrote:

The fight is over, but the work continues. Haven is free, but freedom is fragile. I leave this city in the hands of its people, trusting they will protect it, nurture it, and carry it forward. As for me, I carry the lessons I've learned, the memories of those we lost, and the hope of what lies ahead. This is not an ending. It is a beginning.

A week later, Sophia returned—this time with a group of children. They were students, she explained, part of a new program pairing history with lived experience. Ethan welcomed them with surprise and a warm smile. His quiet cottage was suddenly filled with youthful curiosity.

"Is it true you fought the Overseers?" one boy asked, eyes wide with wonder.

Ethan chuckled and crouched to meet his gaze. "We all fought," he said. "Not just with weapons—but with our voices, our courage, and our belief that things could be better. The Overseers were strong, but we were stronger because we stood together."

A girl with braids pointed to the journal in his hand. "What's in there?"

Ethan looked at the worn cover. "It's not just my story—it's the story of everyone who fought. And one day, it will be yours to tell."

As the sun dipped below the horizon, the children departed, their laughter fading into the evening breeze. That night, Ethan sat by the fire, the journal resting on his lap. His words felt lighter now—no longer burdened by the past, but lifted by the promise of tomorrow.

The resilience of the human spirit is a flame that cannot be extinguished. It flickers. It falters. But it never dies. In the darkest moments, it burns brighter. That is what saved Haven. That is what will carry it forward.

Ethan closed the journal and set it aside. The fire crackled softly beside him. Leaning back in his chair, he gazed up at the stars—clear, untainted by the drones that once filled the skies. Their light spoke of vastness, of freedom, of endless possibility.

He could now hear the birds again. Their songs, once lost beneath mechanical hums, were now a daily chorus of peace.

He thought of Marcus, of Lila, Helena, Sophia, and all the others who shaped the journey. He thought of the crowd in the square that day, their eyes lit with hope. And he thought of the children—their future unburdened by fear.

He wished Marcus were alive to see this. He had fought so hard, only to fall before the sun rose again.

Haven had been reborn—not as a perfect city, but as a place where perfection was no longer the goal. It was a city of humanity—of flaws, of triumphs, of struggle, and of progress.

And that, Ethan thought, was enough.

The next day, Ethan stood on the hill once more. The city stretched out before him, vast and alive. The wind carried voices and laughter through the air.

He opened the journal one last time and wrote:

To those who come after us:

Remember that freedom is not a destination—it's a journey. A path we walk together. A promise we keep for one another. Nurture it. Protect it. And never forget the flames that lit the way.

With a steady hand, he closed the journal and placed it on the shelf beside Marcus's original one. The stories were complete. But the journey was far from over.

For Ethan. For Haven. For generations yet to come.

The future awaited—bright, uncertain, and full of promise.

Maybe he would write a book.

No—he would **definitely** write a book.

The rise and fall of the Overseers would make a powerful story—and an even greater lesson. He knew their shadows still lingered. As long as people like his brother existed, the Overseers would seek to rise again.

But Haven was no longer their haven.

It was now their seed of paradise.

Their seed of Heaven.